BORDERLINES: An American Tragedy

Book I

Casey

"Don't Ever Call Me Worthless"

By Daniel Orr

Dedicated to

The memory of

She who gave me the most joyful time of my life despite the out-come.

Mental Illness is not a choice.

The mentally ill do not choose their behaviors as normal thinking people do. For some it is learned helplessness. They just do without thought or consideration because it's all they know.

It takes more than love. It takes patience and understanding and far too often when the safety of the familiar is in danger they fight against anything new, even when it's better.

Introduction

When people go astray, as they often do when they try to discover who they are as a person, they are often met with a great deal of resistance from people who think they know them better. Usually these people are well intentioned and seasoned people who are ripe with wisdom and experience from their own lives. This is of little consequence to those that they love because life is a personal journey. A journey of exploration that leads each one of us to try and discover what really makes us happy. The truth discovered is often that what makes us happy one day is completely different than what will make us happy tomorrow, or next month, or next year. Another truth discovered is that which makes us unhappy is usually permanent. So the list of bad experiences grows to mold us into beings of aversion. As we pursue happiness we then begin to surround ourselves by not the things that make us happy but by those things that do not bring us discomfort or pain. Some of the people that we know who are always so unhappy are because they are their own source of discomfort. They surround themselves by immediate gratifications that take the focus off of them and onto things external so that can live vicariously instead of creating their own future.

Such is the story about to be told. The story is true and it isn't. Because truth is a perception of the believer. The truth of this story is that every condition is a perception of the obvious from the first and a lot of conclusions toward the end. In no way does it make the story less true but it opens the possibility that all the facts portrayed are perceptual and may in fact not be facts at all. No matter the reading, the story is a story of love that began out of curiosity and one person's belief that everyone should help everyone else if they have the power to do so. A lesson learned from the Lorax – "UNLESS." Dr. Seuss wrote, "Unless someone like you cares a whole awful lot, nothing is going to get better. It's not."

From that noble beginning started a love that would end tragically from this story's perspective. The retelling is mostly therapeutic and hoping that for all that may read it that each and every one of us might find some truth to call their own. To expand their journey and hope that someone might have foresight in a world where hind-sights are the burdens we carry. So that maybe someone can be understanding and preventive instead of scared and reactive.

This is James' story with Casey in it.

October 2010

"You can't save them all, but that doesn't mean you shouldn't try." – Dano Orr

James stood before the mirror painting his face for the Halloween costume contest. It would be the third one he participated in at The Gentlemen's Club. Although beat the year prior by a true dwarf who dressed up with his taller friend as Dr. Evil and Mini-me, James had planned a strategy all year for the thousand dollar prize.

Modeling himself after the movie, *Legend*, James created his own version of Mephistopheles although he was quite certain that the strippers and usual patrons would simply call him the devil or a demon. But it was no matter. Halloween was his favorite holiday of the year. And since he had made it a habit to come and eat with his favorite bartender, he had also come to know all of the waiter staff and most of the exotic dancers. Quite a few of them seemed to like him as well.

Now, James had visited strip clubs when he was in the Navy but that was 25 years ago. Then it was just an easy way to see boobies and underage drinking. But after a quarter century James' life had really changed. His twenty year marriage ended after he developed a disability that required him needing to be cared for instead of being the primary care giver to his family. From the outside, the family looked ideal, all American. Mom stayed home with kids. Dad went off to work. Mom dressed up the children and took them to church and Dad spent Saturday night playing with his friends and their families.

What most people did not see was that behind closed doors things were very different. That James' missus suffered from perfectionism, a type of Obsessive Compulsive Disorder or OCPD. And because the world, especially children, was not perfect the wife stayed depressed on and off, more on than off. But with all her southern graces, she smiled and offered a façade of normality and happiness. The truth was far different.

After James had started becoming ill, he went to the emergency room and his general practitioners. Their diagnosis was that he was forty and over-weight. James argued that he knew lots of fat forty year olds and that they did not complain of his symptoms. But to no immediate avail.

James life would suddenly become very vivid. Because of the unidentified illness, James has an industrial accident. He was hurt badly and would need eighteen months to recover. During this time and for the first time James saw the neglect that his children had endured for fifteen years. True they were clean and clothed and chauffeured. It was true that they had been given individual tasks to entertain them. But what was also true was that the mother's depression and inability to control herself when the world presented itself imperfectly had had a severe impact on the children. James knew his wife's condition as together they had identified it through counseling and found her treatment for it. In fact, life had been so good after the treatment that in two years' time they had decided to expand their family by two more kids.

The additional kids were an easy decision. James had been very successful at managing money and by the age of 38, their home was paid for, their savings and retirement were filling fast. The only concern was that James' wife should stay on her medications for OCPD and depression. But she didn't. She expressed that she didn't want to poison the unborn children. James argued that a happy mother was better for the developing baby than a stressed mother. But James had introduced an element into his family that was against him. As part of James wife's therapy was to become part of a social group. James told Carol, his wife, that she should return to the church of her youth where she had so many family ties. He wanted her to be part of a place where she felt safe and accepted. These ties would introduce more complications than James ever anticipated. The first was that they convinced Carol that her body was a temple to god not to be polluted with the drugs of men. And at first James could not argue because pregnancy had been good to his wife, Carol. Her spirits were high and she was focused and reading about how to take care of an unborn child. Carol always loved nutrition, exercise and physical health.

The only incident worth noting was that, one morning Carol and James were watching the news and a teenager on an antidepressant had stolen a single engine plane and had apparently committed suicide by flying into a sky rise building in Miami. James, who had always been particularly sarcastic, snarked well at least he was original in his suicide method. The commentator on television then introduced an expert guest speaker. The speaker commented on the dangers of giving teens anti-depressants and that it was very common that when someone of any age suddenly stopped taking an SSRI (Serotonin Selective Reuptake Inhibitor) that they became a danger to themselves in various ways. Carol commented that that was true because when she went cold turkey from her Zoloft she heard voices in her head on several occasions. James looked at her odd, "Really?" he asked. Carol nodded that it was true but then went into the kitchen.

So when the second child of the second set of children was born she came into the world early. She came into the world with a cord around her neck and discolored. The doctor ordered the live birth recording to be stopped and immediately took the baby away without showing it to Carol. Carol began crying out for information but they kept working on the baby. It was just a few minutes, maybe two or three, but it seemed like eternity. Then the baby cried and everyone began looking more relieved. The nurse explained to Carol that the baby needed a little extra attention and that she could see her soon. But this was Carol's fourth baby, and she knew this was not normal at all. Something inside snapped and she was never the same again. She never recovered from her post-partum depression. Her symptoms returned for perfectionism OCPD. Only this time she was angry and defensive instead of depressed.

James begged, pleaded, offered readings but Carol claimed it was out of her hands; it was all God's will now. That this life didn't matter. And with the help of her church, Carol's current life didn't matter. She would not take her medications that had worked well so before. She claimed it was polluting her body and she wasn't going to be some drug abuser, that her body was a temple to the Lord.

James tried for six months to get her to go back on her medications and seek counseling again. Carol refused over and over. When Carol began talking fatalistic saying that it was all out of her control and that God would take care of things. That this life didn't matter except to prepare for the next one, that triggered the memory of when Carol stopped taking her meds cold turkey and spoke of hearing voices in her head. James remembered the story of Andrea Yates, the Texas woman that had drowned five of her kids. A newspaper clipping reported the event this way, "*This crime story would unravel in dark and strange ways, with the reasons why a loving mother of five had drowned all of her children tangled in issues of depression, religious fanaticism, and psychosis.*"

James would hire a lawyer and go to the courts and ask them to help Carol get back into treatment. That would be the end of twenty years of marriage. James felt sad and angry but never shed a tear. He was more relieved after having had to work so hard for so long. Even their second born, thirteen at the time, commented that she did not realize how dark the cloud was until it was gone.

James didn't want anyone else in his life. He was tired. He liked hanging out and conversations but he didn't want to have to work at a loveless relationship. He was happy being alone.

Three years later James would meet Casey, the woman who would forever change his world and life. James was unaware that he had never truly been in love before. A romantic love based off of mutual attractions and common interests.

November 2010

Curious at First Sight

"Curiosity killed the cat." - Unknown

Having lost the Costume Contest and suddenly being shunned for his choice of costumes; James decided just to concentrate on the few employees that had incorporated him into their real world social lives. These young ladies mostly worked day shift and James rarely visited in the day. But one of his favorites enticed him because she knew James' true motivation for coming. Lucy told him that a new girl had started working and that she was so weird that all the emotional wrecks, drug addicts, and dysfunctional strippers were pointing her out to be strange. "Strange?" James asked Lucy.

"She's like a zombie" commented Lucy. "She stares at you for inappropriate lengths of time and then it seems as if she just looks through you." Lucy shook her head and twirled her finger to indicate she thought the girl was crazy.

"What's her name?" James asked.

"Her dancer name is Jewel. I don't know her real name. Don't wanna know her at all." Lucy went back to her duties and James decided he would have to visit the dayshift.

The next day James went to the Gentleman's Club for the buffet lunch only to discover they had discontinued that event. He sat down in the middle of the strip club and realized how big it was and how empty it seemed in the day time. He was one of just three customers and there was at least a dozen strippers waiting to pounce. The waitresses being his friends seemed to divert them away which was good because James didn't buy dances anyway. Lucy came by and plopped down next to him. "Didn't expect to see you so soon."

"I came to see this zombie girl you told me about." James replied.

Lucy looked around the room and then

nodded toward the far bar. "There she is sitting at the end of the bar." James' waitress walks up and hears Lucy pointing out Jewel.

"She's probably waiting to steal more cigarettes out of our drawer. I have told them to tell her to stay out of our drawer that is for the waitresses. The dancers have their own lockers." Like most of the girls that worked at the strip club, Alice had her own issues, and she had been slow to warm up to James. But after a few months of hanging out in the same group she had come to accept him if not like him a little. James ordered a drink and asked for a dinner menu. Alice trotted off to get his requests.

James couldn't really tell a lot about the new girl, Jewel. They all seemed tall in their eight inch heels. And she didn't seem so zombie like walking around the bar in the distance and in the dark. A second waitress walked up and hugged James. "What'cha durin?" asked Amy.

"I was checking out the new girl" said

James.

"Something wrong with her. She just stares through walls most of the time and you should see her dance." Amy was chewing gum like she was trying to destroy evidence. James looked up at her and smiled. Skinny little thing that claimed she just needed money to pay for school. That was the most common lie told by dancers but not usually one told by the waitresses. Amy was different however. She did not complain about where she worked or her life. She just talked about finishing school and opening a day care center. James liked her because she seemed very grounded and focused for an eighteen year old. "She is supposed to dance in a minute; they called her name out to be next."

Lucy snorted, "Wait till you see her. She's an odd one." Lucy checked her phone and then set her clip board on the table. She was the rub girl that day and for $10 for three minutes she would work your shoulder muscles quite nicely. She had the best hands and James often told her she needed to look into being a professional masseuse.

James reached down and looked at her clip board. Two customers three rubs. Lucy wasn't making much money today. James put twenty five dollars on the board. "Two songs and a tip, whenever you're ready."

Lucy smiled. She knew he would buy a rub as he always did. "I'll be right back. Watch my stuff." Lucy departed and James scanned the room for the dancer named Jewel.

Such an assortment of people was in here even in the day time. There was the Russian Girl who was much older than most of them and seemed to only entertain people she had made relationships with. She never chased a new face. And apparently she only worked three days a week and supplemented that income with stripper thongs that she made with sequins. One pair she sold for twenty five dollars. That amazed James and he considered making some himself just to see if it could be profitable. But then another stripper in the place explained why she sold so many pair of thongs. There was a busting market for worn thongs. Apparently, customers would often buy an exotic dancer's underwear for $50 to $100 dollars so they could take them home and smell them or wear them or whatever fantasy they might have. This seemed a little extreme to James, and although he considered it for a moment, it just didn't seem like anything he would enjoy. The music changed, the stripper on the stage picked up her clothes and moved to the stairs behind the stage.

Jewel walked out on stage. The first song the dancer always remained clothed. She was not very tall and she moved rather slow and nervous. Walking to the center of the stage she grabbed the brass pole and walked around it like a half-hearted parade. She moved from one side of the stage to the other, and that's when James noticed the first interesting thing about her. Although she was not performing well as a dancer, she was walking with poise. She stood erect, shoulders rolled back. At first he wondered if she was just trying to make her breasts seem larger but as the music changed to the next song, Jewel took her dress off and folded it and then set it on the floor. "Folded her dress," James observed. "That's unusual."

Lucy returned, unbuttoned James shirt, and squirted some Jergen's lotion in her hands. As she began kneading his muscles like some benevolent goddess, she leaned forward pressing her breasts against his head and whispered in his good ear, "That's her." James nodded. Topless Jewel paraded slowly around the stage like a frightened slave. She had not needed to roll her shoulder's back to make her breasts look bigger as they were of ample size naturally. Jewel turned and then turned again, and as she did, she covered one breast and then the other. Something seemed odd about her performance, and then James surmised that she was modest.

James leaned his head back to look up at Lucy, "Watch her. She only exposes one breast at a time. She hides the other." Lucy and James watched as Jewel did just that. One of the customers stood and walked to the stage. Jewel let her hands down and walked down to him. James smiled; even from the distance you could tell that one boob was just slightly larger than the other. Not in an ugly way but a beautiful natural way. He wondered was that the reason she hid one breast and then the other? Was she modest to be naked on a stage, or was she embarrassed because her boobs didn't match perfectly.

Amy and Alice both returned to James small table at the same time. Setting down his menu and Ice Tea, Alice commented again about not supposed to get tea out of the lounge because it wasn't for customers. Made sense of course, sober customers don't spend as much money. James smiled at Alice, and she scampered off to other things. "What do you think of her?" asked Amy.

"I don't know. She seems very out of place." said James.

"She seems from outer space if you ask me," said Lucy. Amy laughed and nodded. James offered his knee and Amy sat down. James pointed out all the things he had noticed. How she had folded her dress instead of tossing it on the stairs like the other girls. How she walked upright and with poise like someone had taught her some social etiquette.

Then he asked both women, "Do you think she's modest, and that's why she covers one breast and then the other, or do you think she's embarrassed that one is slightly larger than the other." Amy admitted that she hadn't really noticed, and Lucy professed that she didn't really care. But James was intrigued because this girl was the outcast of all these women that had their own sets of drama and issues. Yet they all seemed to agree that Jewel was an exception even among the exceptions. James looked at

Amy and handed her a five dollar bill. "Go tip her on stage and tell her I would like for her to have lunch with me." Amy took the money and did as requested. Jewel bent down to listen to Amy and looked into the darkness to try and find the customer she referred to.

Lucy was rubbing James neck for the fourth song now as Jewel walked up the stairs on the back of the stage. He always wondered if he should pay her more or just let her spoil him. Since she was pretty much guaranteed twenty five dollars a week from him, he decided to just keep enjoying his bonus. Now an outsider looking in would think that a few extra rubs was not really worth the twenty five dollars a month, but then again, they didn't see the whole picture. Lucy knew, like Svetlana the night time bartender, that James really just liked to talk and watch people. And that naked women with issues and drama was better than any television show ever produced. James had earned a reputation for leading girls away from the club for better lives.

Add to that that twice a month Lucy would invite him to be at a club she would be attending that week. Most people would quickly assume that she just wanted to tap into his pockets and have the forty three year old man buy the twenty two year old woman her drinks. But quite the opposite happened. At the local bars down on the college drag, guys would buy Lucy drinks for just a few moments of conversation time. Lucy would walk the room, and as her drinks began to accumulate, she would walk over and sit with James and hand them to him. He got to drink for free and enjoy the company of a girl that seemed by far the most interesting and was an exotic beauty on top of that. Sometimes James would comment that when he made his millions, he would have Lucy live with him in a pool house and her job would simply be to tan, rub his shoulders, and talk to him when he was sitting about the pool. Lucy would laugh and tell him that she would take the job.

When Jewel walked over to the table,

Lucy decided to stop rubbing his shoulders. She scratched James head because she knew how much he loved it and then picked up her clip board and walked away. James stood up and pulled out a chair for Jewel. She looked at him queer and then sat down. Not wasting a moment she asked him, "Would you like for me to dance for you?"

James laughed, "I don't buy dances. I just come here to eat and talk." Jewel's face kept her disinterested expression, and she pushed her chair back as if to stand. "Wait. Please have lunch with me. You have to eat don't you?" Jewel glared at him and James handed her the menu. "Choose whatever you like." Jewel seemed very distant which is exactly how all the girls had described her. She took the menu and she began reading and James watched and waited. Her eyes would scan the menu and then pause. James wondered what she was considering. He patiently waited and then realized she was still staring at one space on the menu. "Do you see something you like?"

Jewel looked up at him and then back down to the menu. She resumed scanning the menu and then spoke, "I think I would like to have the Jambalaya." James heart began to beat faster. The zombie girl had just picked his favorite dish off the menu.

"It's pretty spicy, as in hot, most people don't like that, but it is my favorite."

Jewel looked up at him and didn't smile, "I eat spicy foods. I prefer them." Not a lot of warmth in her tone but she had picked a dish from the fare that so few would dare eat. He couldn't wait to watch and see how she handled it.

Jewel listened as James described different things like the costume contest and how the waitresses had adopted him into their social lives. He was very appreciative that they had given him something to do rather than stay home all the time. However anytime he asked her any questions Jewel gave vague answers or redirected the questions. She wasn't giving out any information.

When it was obvious that she needed to go and make some money, James thanked her for having dinner. "I do hope you will join me again soon. I don't suppose I could persuade you to tell me your real name?" Jewel had started smiling a little but only briefly. Her lip curled and she shook her head no.

James couldn't wait to see Jewel again. Something was definitely different about this one. He had spent all that night and the next day just wondering what type of person she might be and why she acted the way she did. The waitresses had been right, she was different.

He woke up early that morning eager and curious. James drove his second born to school and then went home and showered and trimmed his beard. His hair was still a bit blue from Halloween. Looking around he saw the cologne his brother insisted that he wear. Maybe it would help? Clean, trimmed, and cologne, James drove the hour back to the strip club just to see Jewel and hopefully have lunch with her again.

When he arrived, she was busy with a customer. Alice sat next to him and chatted about what a pain in the ass Jewel was and that she had stolen someone's thong underware. Now James had no idea if this was or wasn't true, but he did know that the girls here often created drama and lies on a regular basis. But still there was a unified opposition to this Jewel girl.

When her customer got up and left, Jewel walked over to the waitresses' drawer and took something out and walked away. James laughed as Alice exclaimed, "Did you see that bitch in our stuff again!" Alice hopped up and ran to talk to the floor manager. He was a sixty year old floor man that looked like he could care less if the world stopped rotating at any moment. He listened as Alice fussed and pointed and ranted. Amy came by and asked James what was going on, and he told her the dirt. Amy said she had heard that the new girl had stolen someone's clothes.

"Not under-wear?" James asked.

"I heard it was a dress but maybe under-wear." Amy wrinkled her nose, "Who would want to steal someone else's under-ware?" James shrugged and asked for her to get him a menu and to tell Jewel he wanted her to eat with him again.

Jewel came over and immediately asked him if he wanted a dance. James shook his head and pointed to the seat. "I am never going to be your customer, Jewel. I am going to try and find a way for you to trust me enough to let me to take you out to dinner one day. Have you ever been to the Twisted Fork? They serve ostrich. Ever had ostrich?" Jewel shook her head no and then told him that she had already eaten and started to get up. "Please sit with me, if only for a moment." Jewel protested and walked away. She circled the room and Amy brought James a club sandwich and fries.

"She's not going to eat with you?" asked Amy.

"She said she already had eaten."

"Not unless she did it before she came to work." Amy commented that she had forgotten James liked to drown his fries in black pepper, mustard and Tabasco then ran to the kitchen to get him some. Jewel circled the club twice and offered everyone a dance but no takers. She eventually came over and sat next to James.

"Would you like a bite or can I have them bring you something?"

"May I have a few of your fries?" asked Jewel.

"Of course if you can find one not painted with tabasco." James smiled and slid the plate closer to her. Jewel picked up a fry and looked at James. "I have been watching you. You walk like a debutante, like someone who has taken dance or gymnastics."

Jewel pursed her lips and then nodded. "Both." She replied.

"No offense but you seem very out of place here. This is new to you I guess."

"I have been here almost a month. I just got a new place." James realized he had just gotten the first real information out of her. Not much of course but it was something to work from.

"Have you moved in yet? I have a van if you need help moving things around. I am trustworthy. You can ask any of the girls."

"My friend is helping me move. We will be fine." James tried to conceal his disappointment. Usually a friend meant that a pretty girl had a boyfriend. James would discover this was no different but then again it was completely different. If only he had a crystal ball.

James decided that he needed to let

her move and not seem too eager. Something about her was very different. She walked like someone with training and ate like someone from a wealthy family that used etiquette. But she was also very easily distracted. A lull in the conversation and she would gaze off into the distance, as if in a trance, and James would nudge her to snap her back to him.

Three days later, James decided to go back and have lunch again. This time she seemed eager to see him, and she came over without having to be requested. James asked her to sit down and she asked him, "Do I get to dance for you today?"

James smiled at her, "No. I told you. I will never be your customer because I want you to go out with me for all the right reasons." She sat down and had lunch. They talked about the trumpet and band camps. She gave a glimpse of her world fifteen years prior but still it was an opening into who she might really be. James listened and talked and she seemed interested in listening to him as well. Finally, he asked her, "So could I get you to come and go four wheeling with me tomorrow?"

"I have to work," Jewel replied.

"How much money do you make on a Tuesday really?"

"About $200. Not much."

James laughed. "Only $200 really, well. Maybe I am in the wrong profession. I had to learn a lot and work hard for $300 a day and you have to smile and be beautiful and show your boobies for $200 a day. Hardly seems fair." Jewel smiled and flipped her hair back stereotypically as if to tease. "Ok, how about this then. How do I break it down? You don't have to sacrifice $200 to spend a day with me. I'll give it to you to skip work. But I am torn because I am not hiring you to spend the day with me, but then again, I can't see how I am not bribing you either."

Jewel shook her head no and smiled. "How about this. Here is $200 dollars to cover a Tuesday. Call me if you want to and if you don't - don't." James handed her his phone number written on the back of his lunch card. Jewel took the money and stuffed it in her dress. "But at least tell me your real name."

"Why do you insist on knowing my real name?"

"Because it's real and I don't want to know Jewel. I want to take 'real name' out to dinner or go carting or four wheeling or something fun."

"I'll give you a hint. It's the name of a flower."

"A flower?" James shook his head and kissed her hand. "The name of a flower would not do justice to the beauty I see in you." Holding her hand firmly he pulled her a little closer. "If instead of a day, you can only manage an hour, then text me before six and I will meet you at the twisted fork for dinner tonight. But if you want to spend the day, call me."

When James got home he googled 'girl names' against 'flower names' and came up with very few choices. Perhaps, he thought it was just another red herring that strippers do to throw guys off their real lives. He was feeling stupid because he had given her $200. That was not something he had ever done before. He decided not to give it to much thought and just wait and see if she would call. Of course, six o'clock rolled around and she had not called or texted. The next morning he woke up and took his daughter to school and then drove the hour back to see the girl that everyone was still complaining about but that was communicating friendly with him. The two versions did not seem to match. On the way there he got a phone call, and had to make a diversion and go to the vocational rehab office in Raleigh.

His disease was getting better but he still had some issues and he couldn't find anyone who would give him a job because every human resources department would claim he was uninsurable. Where he really wanted to be was with Jewel eating lunch and prying out that next tiny bit of information. As luck would have it, he became free just in time to drive back an hour to get his daughter from school and set her up for the night, and then he took off again and drove an hour back to Raleigh to get to the Men's Club just as she was getting off work. He rushed in and took her hand and said "I have had a long and messed up day. Tell me your name and take me to the private dance room." Jewel took his open hand and squeezed it.

"Heather." She smiled. James didn't believe her not even a little bit. When she was evasive or lying, tiny lines appeared in the corners of her eyes. Different than when she laughed.

She led him into the private dance room and started to take off her clothes.

James stopped her and said "Come here. Just sit. I don't buy dances. I have already seen you naked on stage and if you offer me a booby, I want it to be because you want too."

"I want to dance." Jewel/Heather replied.

"I don't. Sit. Lay your head on my shoulder." She refused. She danced anyway and when she climbed over him, James took her and held her tight and hugged her until she submitted and laid her head on his shoulder. Three minutes and thirty dollars later, she stood up. James said, "Thank you. Oh, and you never called or texted or had dinner or anything except to take the $200, but here is $30 dollars for this time. I wish you would just call me."

Jewel/Heather followed him out and as he turned for the door, she took his arm and said, "I could use some help hanging pictures and curtains this weekend."

James smiled, "Saturday? Around

lunch?" Jewel/Heather nodded. "May I have your phone number?" She looked reluctant and then she grabbed a pen from the bar and wrote it on a napkin. James knew it was fake, but he said thank you anyway.

On his way home, he texted the number and said "Thanks for the trust. See you this weekend." An hour later, he received a reply "OK." James snickered, "Ok?" he wondered. Ok for the trust. Or Ok for the weekend? But he was elated because either way, she had given him her real phone number.

FRIENDSHIP

"A true friend walks in when the rest of the world walks out."

When Saturday rolled around, she had not called nor texted, or even given directions. He had a general idea from what she had said about where he expected her to live so at ten in the morning James began driving towards that locale. He texted, as he left his house, saying he was headed in that direction and then again saying he had arrived at Hwy 70 closer to Durham and needed to know where he was supposed to be.

Jewel/Heather called him and told him he was way off from where she lived and he laughed and said "If you would just give me an address, the GPS will take me straight there." She did and while he had driven twenty extra minutes away he would eventually arrive.

She was amiable but seemed distant,

uncomfortable that he was there but wanting the human contact. The first thing he noticed was several of the boxes had the name Casey written on them. James smiled and decided that he just wouldn't call her anything at all.

She began by saying she had changed her minds about curtains but that she wanted these poster pictures hanging in different places. He obliged her and hammered in hardware to hold the heavy paintings. She had him hang a medicine cabinet and then a letter organizer. In the organizer were a ton of bills all addressed to Casey and several of them were forwarded from more than one address. Obviously she had moved a lot in the recent past.

She asked if he would set up her computer and he did but discovered that her mouse was not working well. She said it was broken, but James pointed out that the light was not on so an optical mouse couldn't work if the batteries were dead. "Do you happen to have any AA batteries?" James asked.

She thought for a moment and then said, "Not new ones. Let me get the ones out of my vibrator." James jerked his head back and smirked. Not that he was surprised she had a battery operated boyfriend but that she so openly just tossed it out there. Bringing him the batteries he seemed awkward accepting them considering where they had been.

After placing them in the mouse, the light came on and in a moment was working on the screen as well. "See. Sometimes the simplest solution is the right one."

"I need to get some things for the apartment," Jewel/Heather/Casey commented. "So I will have to leave and go to Wal-Mart."

James smiled. "Are you telling me that it's time for me to go or that you want me to go shopping with you?" She thought for a moment and then nodded. James smiled at her because to him that wasn't an answer to a two part question so he decided to make it the second half of the question and so he sat on her red Naugahyde couch and looked at National Geographic magazine that featured New York on the cover.

Jewel/Heather/Casey disappeared in her bedroom and took a shower. She emerged with a towel wrapped around her small frame and a towel wrapped around her hair. She went into the kitchen and looked for something but never actually picked anything up. James sat on the couch and watched her. She seemed indifferent to his presence but paused to make sure he noticed she was so vulnerable in just a towel. "Will you be long?" he asked.

"I have to get ready. You don't have to stay unless you just want too."

"I do want to, if you will allow me." James countered. She smiled and cleaned her ear out with a Q-tip. Then she disappeared into her bedroom again.

Over two hours would pass before she was actually ready to leave for the store. James had been very patient but then again what would he do. Jewel/Heather/Casey had finally let him into her real world and he was very very pleased. She didn't act any differently at home than she did in the club. She was still as distant and prone to long pauses staring through the walls as if lost in thought. Finally she announced she was ready, and they headed to the front door. As soon as James opened it, Casey said "hold on" and disappeared around the hall. James waited about thirty seconds and then followed her.

She was standing in the second hallway shaking, tears rolling down her cheeks. James opened his arms and walked to her slowly and then wrapped her up. He ran his hand across her shoulders and squeezed her tightly. "I don't know who hurt you so deeply but I promise I never will. Not on purpose. I will never hurt you." The hug lasted several minutes, and then he let her go and walked into her room and brought her a tissue.

They made it to Wal-Mart and Jewel/Heather/Casey took the cart down the first row. James felt a little out of place. He had never given it any real thought, but suddenly he realized that grocery shopping was a very intimate affair. As Jewel/Heather/Casey walked down each aisle, she selected things she wanted or needed and placed them in the cart. One of her first selections was ice cream.

James often wondered why Wal-Mart placed ice cream so near the front of the store. Was it because they wanted people to buy it on their way out or for some other psychological marketing reason?

Aisle by aisle she shopped, stopping frequently to analyze categories of products. She would pick up each item and read its nutritional label and then choose another and compare the two. Often she would stop comparing and look through the can, through the shelf and off into some other dimension of time and space. James stood at the end of the aisle not to be intrusive. He noticed she had disappeared into what he was beginning to think were anxiety attacks. She was disassociating. He walked down the aisle and began a conversation but it wasn't till he touched her that it seemed to snap her back into the present.

Looking into her cart, James could not help but be his observant self. Most of the items she had selected were not complete meal choices. She was buying by what she liked and not planning a dinner plan for multiple days. It was all impulse shopping. But then again, her cupboards were completely bare so perhaps that was what she needed to do. Begin with what she liked most and fill in the gaps as they became more apparent. Curiously, however, he noted that more often than not she was choosing not only the same products he would have chosen but the same brands. This commonality seemed a random coincident that made him wonder was she perhaps compatible with him from a food stand point. She did after all look a very large menu and then select his favorite fare from it. Jambalaya that sounds good right now.

The whole shopping experience ended with choosing a microwave oven. There were about ten choices. James thought perhaps that was seven too many. A good marketer would have had three brands and they would represent small, mid, and large microwaves. By limiting the choices purchasers would only have to decide what size they wanted and was it a brand they could trust. By offering so many choices, the decision to buy a microwave was reduced because now consumers felt like they had to research all the models. What could this one do that that one couldn't? Was one with a rack better than one with a turntable? Is there one that you could have metal in without all the pops and snaps. On top of this James is now watching Jewel/Heather/Casey try and decide which microwave she wanted.

After thirty minutes of casual perusing she began to study the attributes of each model. James looked at the ice cream melted and now dripping out of the bottom of the grocery cart. Pointing this out to her, he flipped the container over to prevent any more mess and then tried to help her by narrowing her choices eliminating certain ones and making a strong case for only three. His diversion worked that her focus narrowed; however it would still be another half hour before she decided, and he placed it on the shopping cart and rolled it to the check-out line.

Putting all the food away and setting up the microwave went very quickly. Jewel/Heather/Casey talked about needing to buy a washer and dryer, and that she was going to have to go to the laundry mat and clean her clothes. James told her to use his machines. He sold her on the idea stating that she had to eat, so while she did laundry he would make her dinner. That by using his machines she could save money in quarters, get a free meal and he could return the favor of trust. She had allowed him to know where she lived so he said, "It would be only fair if you knew where I lived."

She accepted this idea hesitantly but seemed to make it much faster than any of the other decisions she had been faced with so far. She loaded up four loads of laundry and he carried them out to his van. He drove her to his home an hour away.

When they arrived, he carried a laundry basket to the front door and placed the key in the lock then paused. Turning to look at the beautiful younger woman on his doorstep he could not help but grin, "Before you come into my house I need to know something." She looked perplexed and confused, perhaps even taken aback a bit. "Tell me your name? I need to know who is coming into my house."

She rolled her eyes, "You know my name already. You saw it in my house."

"Maybe, but you never told me your name. I want you to introduce yourself to me." He held out his hand to shake hers, "Hi. I am James."

Smiling bright and wide, "I am Casey."

"Pleased to meet you, Casey. Won't you come in?"

GRATITUDE

"If the only prayer you said was thank you, that would be enough."
— *Meister Eckhart*

Laundry was done and girl returned safely home without being assaulted or kidnapped. James returned to visit her Sunday evening. She had claimed to have finished unpacking everything although the second bedroom had a number of unopened boxes.

Her ambitious project for the evening was to sort and match socks. Hundreds, well at least it seemed that way and there also seemed to be no matches.

Interestingly at the club the waitresses had accused her of stealing underwear. Now James was not sure what type of person would steal another's underwear for the purpose of clothing. James found it oddly satisfying to see on the corner of her dresser packaging from a store where she had bought thongs. He was amazed at their costs, but since the waitresses had referenced that another dancer had hand sewn the ones in question, seeing the package was a relief.

The two of them sat on the floor and they did what would become the most wonderful of activities between them. Casey and James talked. They laughed and snorted and giggled and smiled. They were not trying to be impressive or silly; they were just being themselves while sorting socks that had no matches.

Their personalities came out as well. James lined socks in categories and rows by color, size and thickness. Casey picked up one from one pile and moved it to another back and forth like some Chinese Puzzle. Occasionally James would catch a glimpse of a sock that looked like it should fit in one of his organized patterns. He would steal it from Casey's piles. Casey did not object to his system; she just laughed every time he rearranged things into new sub groups.

James commented on one of her rings. Casey said it was a birthday present and so he asked, "When was your birthday?" She told him it was in October, but this year not a single soul had remembered or acknowledged. James found that to be very sad. He could see the pain in her face as she tried to change the topic to something that was not about her.

Interestingly, she didn't have a panic attack at all that night. She seemed alert and filled with mirth. After an hour of futile sorting, James announced that this project was done and began tossing things in a basket. Casey objected but he countered with, "when we find more socks we will try again." Then he stood up and took her hand. "Let's eat something."

She commented that she wasn't really hungry but she got ready all the same. James told her they weren't going out for a night on the town; they were going for something simple. She took the hint and they went casual. When they walked out the door Casey paused. A look of confusion and then panic, turning the door knob she looked at James, "I locked myself out."

"Does the landlord live in the complex? Can you get another key this late?"

Casey looked at him blankly as if she wanted to say something that she didn't want to. "There is another key. We can go get it."

James shrugged his shoulders, "OK. Where do we need to go?" They got in the van and she pointed out directions exactly when they needed to turn. James smiled and shook his head, "It would help if you gave me a little warning." Casey seemed very apprehensive about this trip. James sensing the tension but did not emphasize anything hoping to relieve whatever she was hiding.

"Stop here. This is my friend's house."

"Want me to wait?"

"Yes," she answered quickly. She walked down the driveway and knocked on the door. A figure emerged and after a brief exchange she stepped inside. She wasn't in the house long before hastily walking up the path.

"Everything ok?" James asked. Casey looked at the floor and nodded. James took that to imply, "please don't ask anything else."

After a sub sandwich, he took her home. She opened the door and walked into the darkness. He followed a few steps behind her, and she laid out her pocket book on the table. Finding her keys, Casey looked as if she was inventorying her belongings.

James walked over and took her by the shoulders. "It's gonna be ok." He hugged her tightly. "It's late. You need some rest." Casey looked at him and then said to follow.

She sat out on her deck and lit a cigarette. "That was George. I lived with him for about a month; he helped me get this place because I needed a co-signer." She puffed on the cigarette, her delicate hands trembling.

He had helped her get her own place so there couldn't have been too much bad blood between them. James leaned against a wall and watched her. She avoided making eye contact. She told him that she was working at a sandwich shop and that George had found her there and took her in when she had nowhere else to live. James wondered had she been living out of her car or with someone else, but he figured she would tell him if she wanted to. He was actually just very pleased that the walls were coming down. The story was simple and vague. Casey felt George wanted more than she could give him and had become more expectant. He suggested she find new housing, and she told him she had no money. George recommended she take a job as a stripper and after making enough money to rent her own place, which is what she had done with his help.

Casey was looking into another dimension. It had been a while since James saw this disassociation. He wondered if she was just contemplating but she was lost. The cigarette in her hand was burning away slowly. James shifted and watched her, then moved slowly in front of her to see if she ever focused on him but she didn't. He wasn't sure how long she had been silent or how long he had been studying her, but looking at the cigarette, it had burned all the way down. James spoke sharply, "Casey! You ok, honey?"

"I don't like it there. I don't like the people." Casey took another draw from her cigarette and realized there was nothing left. She then stuffed it into an empty juice glass filled with previous smokes. James walked over and knelt down in front of her.

Taking her hands, he looked up at her and smiled. "It's going to be ok. You will figure it out. I'll help if you want me to as much as I can." He squeezed her hands to reassure her and then stood up and kissed her forehead. "I have to go home. Get some sleep."

FLIRITATION

"It is the same in love as in war, a fortress that parleys is half taken." – Marquerite De Valois

The third date began long before James saw Casey. He now knew that she was brand new to being a stripper. In her telling of her stay with George, Casey indicted she had meet someone that had been a stripper and made a lot of money fast from time to time. Seemingly it was something of a necessity to get Casey's life back into her own control as it seemed to be very broken before George.

James thought only that she just needed a little positive reassurance that life is what you make of it. And true to James' nature he does what he always does. He spoils the person he is with. Not a romantic gesture and nothing sexist. James just had a tendency to spoil people and be overly helpful. Altruistic, he gained his happiness through giving to others.

She needed socks, because he didn't

want to match another sock ever. So he went to Target and he searched out socks. Toe socks, thick socks, athletic socks, he had not realized how much socks cost but it didn't really matter. He found some soccer socks for his older daughter and toe socks for his little ones. Then he saw the Hello Kitty socks.

James thought, Casey had a few Hello Kitty knick knacks but no-where to put them. So he went to Lowes and got a small corner display case and shelf. They weren't much to look at but they were on clearance for only $25. "I will call it a birthday present, one month late" he thought. A birthday she didn't have this year. He had bought socks yesterday and the shelves today, so what else do you need for a birthday? A cake! James went to the baker and picked out a sheet cake and decorated it with Hello Kitty stuff that would make any six year old girl squeal with excitement. He hoped she would appreciate it even though her birthday was a month past. Texting her, he asked if he could come over when she got off work and she said she'd like that. James could hardly contain himself. A friend had entered his life. Someone to go to the movies with or out to eat with, but more so than any other of his friends, this new one seemed to really want him to be around often.

He met her at the door when she came home. Seeing the cake and flowers and gift bags, her eyebrow shot up like quizzical and queer. "How long have you been waiting she asked?"

"Not too long. I didn't want the ice cream cake to melt."

"Why did you do all that?" Casey seemed judgmental and suddenly stand offish, but it did not put James off.

Smiling he said, "To me, birthdays are sacred. They are a celebration of another trip around the sun. And we only get so many trips. You said no one remembered your birthday. But they should have. I wanted you to have a birthday this year even if it was late."

When Casey saw the Hello Kitty decoration, her face lit up bright. James could have stopped right there, but the party had to continue even if it was just the two of them. First he set out the shelves and told her he would build them tomorrow (basically inviting himself back). She did not object and then she opened the bag and saw dozens of socks. She looked up at him startled almost. "Really?"

James laughed, "It's a boy solution. Throw those other socks away, too much work. I found you everything you talked about needing except black socks. And your feet are tiny."

"You shouldn't have done all this." Casey looked sad suddenly.

James walked over and wrapped his arms around her. "I do exactly as I want. And today I wanted you to have a birthday party. Just enjoy it, it won't last long." He cut the cake, and she nibbled at it, but wouldn't really eat it. Then her cell phone buzzed and she looked at it and set it aside. "You can answer it. I don't mind." She shook her head no.

They talked about past birthday parties. Casey thanked him and told him how much she loved Hello Kitty and Sanrio assuming he had knowledge, but he laughed at her and pointed out that he didn't know anything about Sanrio or Hello Kitty. Casey expanded the conversation to include cartoons and anime. This he had second hand knowledge of. His second daughter loved anime. So although he knew very little of the details, he could prime the conversation with the different titles that he had spoiled his daughter with.

Casey seemed very happy. The happiest yet, in fact, and she asked him would he like to stay and watch a movie. "Of course I would." The two of them sat on her red Naugahyde couch and wrapped up in a blanket that smelled of mothballs. They didn't snuggle or cuddle but they were under the same wrapping enjoying the same event. James had not had a friend to share with in a very long time. They could have been watching paint dry and he would have been just as happy.

Then there was a knock at the door. Casey took a deep breath and looked as if it were not entirely unexpected. James wondered if he had been setup to be there except that he knew he had asked to come over. Casey seemed to know the event was coming but not to realize that it was going to happen then. George came in. He and Casey talked in the foyer and then he came and got his chairs from around her shabby little table.

"Would you like some help?" James offered George. Casey cut her eyes at him as if to say stay out of it.

"No, thank you," replied George. He took the chairs and the two of them disappeared outside for just a few minutes. Eventually, she came back to the couch and she sat a little closer and set her hand on James' knee.

"I'm sorry." She offered.

"No worries, boo."

"Boo? Don't call me that." Casey seemed very offended.

"Sorry Hun. No disrespect intended. Just I have a lot of daughters, and it just comes out that way sometimes, most of the time."

"Well, I am not a Boo." James smirked and nodded. There was no reason to argue. She was already primed to fight over whatever happened between her and George. James refused to let her have an opening to inappropriately direct her hostilities. The movie played, but she was distracted. James was deaf and couldn't hear the movie anyway. "I'm sorry but I am not feeling my best," Casey said. She got up and walked into her bedroom and then came back out with a pillow. "If you would like to sleep on the couch that would be ok." James didn't over analyze. Whether she needed him to feel safe or welcome or was worried about him driving home, none of that mattered. She had invited him to stay, and he was both elated and extremely fearful.

James was fearful because he would snore so loud that he could peel back paint and then slam it back in place again. His friends of twenty years hated to share a hotel suite with him, even when they had separate rooms. James had just made this friend he didn't want to lose her because he snored like a train.

Plus that couch, even folded out, was the most uncomfortable bed he had slept on since the navy. The blanket smelled like mothballs so his eyes watered. But you couldn't have moved him if you had tried. The next morning he got up early and went down to the grocery store and bought breakfast items. Returning back to her apartment, he met her with breakfast and flowers.

She seemed grumpy and not a morning person at all, but she also seemed happy to find him still there. "I have to go to work soon. Did you leave my door open when you went to the grocery store?"

James shirked, "I left it unlocked but not open and I was only gone about 15 minutes. Unless you have a stalker you should be safe."

"I have had a stalker before," she said flatly.

James didn't know what to say but decided redirection was worth a shot. "I was going to stay and build the cabinet shelf and corner case before I left. If that's ok?" She didn't answer right away instead looking at him with intensity and thought. She walked away and looked at the little table. Her eyes traced it and she looked perturbed. She paced outside and smoked and then went to her bedroom. James stood in the kitchen and just let her have her space. It was after all her space, her apartment, her life. When she didn't emerge from the bedroom, James announced himself and after a delay walked around the hall into the door of her bedroom. She was sitting on the edge of the bed, tears running down her face.

James walked in and sat on the floor in front of her. "Every day will get better. One day at a time. Get ready for work. Text me or call me anytime."

"Don't ever leave my door open again." Casey spoke sternly to him. James pursed his lips and nodded. He was not nearly as paranoid, but then again, he didn't live in the city in an apartment. But he was sure he had violated some rule. Casey held out her hand and gave him the key to her apartment that George had previously had. "Lock up when you leave." James agreed that he would.

ABSENSE

The Heart soon forgets what the eyes see not. - Unknown

James had his daughters over the weekend and so he didn't visit Casey Friday through Sunday. They had spent about every other day with one another having endless conversations. They both talked and laughed and shared. James loved the time with his kids, but he could not wait to get back and see Casey again. Talking to her Sunday, she invited him over to watch another movie after he took his girls back to their mothers.

When he arrived she seemed almost disinterested, as if the three days absent had reset everything. She was tense and put off. He did not want to pry figuring if she wanted to let him know, she would. Looking around the apartment he saw that it was untidy. There was Chinese takeout on the coffee table and several glasses here and there.

"I wish I had known you were eating

Chinese tonight, I would have had you get me some."

"That was from Friday." she responded flatly. Now that was a red flag for James. She left food out on a table for two days? He picked up dishes and trash carrying them to the kitchen. He could not help but wonder what would let a person leave trash and debris around like that. But then again, nothing about Casey was conventional. She seemed to really be out of it today. Their usual banter was just not happening. She seemed annoyed that he was cleaning her apartment and so he stopped.

"What movie did you want to watch? I brought some." She chose the comedy and they wrapped up together on the couch, this time each of them with their own blanket. Now James liked this movie but could not get the speakers loud enough for his disabled hearing. He changed his position to get his head closer to the speakers. He didn't notice at first but Casey seemed annoyed that he was not aligned with her. When he did notice, he pointed out his deafness again and then reached out his arm. Casey crawled under it and snuggled against him loosely and quickly fell asleep. James had seen this movie a dozen times; his interest in it was gone now. All he could do was watch her sleep next to him. She is so beautiful and so unpredictable.

James thought back over the last two weeks. The waitresses had called her a zombie and drug addict. They were partially right. She was often paralyzed by anxiety and she seemed to take a lot of over the counter pain killers. James looked over to the kitchen. There was no alcohol in her house. He recalled seeing anxiety medication in her bedroom when they were doing the socks. They were prescribed to her and seemed dated if he remembered correctly and were in a basket, not in a place where they might be taken regularly.

Maybe something had happened over

the weekend with George. James looked up at the rickety kitchen table that looked like it came from a thrift store and was the only choice.

He bit his lip. They had not talked today and he missed that. But here she was spooned against him and sleeping soundly. James wanted to stay all night with her but knew he needed to be at home with his oldest daughter and take her to school in the morning. She would get her license in two weeks and then she really would be independent. He was going to miss taking care of her. Being her chauffer and spoiling her friends with buffet spreads at their anime events and soccer practices.

James lifted himself up as gently as he could but he still woke Casey up. She asked what he was doing, and he told her he needed to go home. She said bye and walked to her bedroom. James picked up his keys and put on his shoes. Everyone is entitled to a bad day. He wondered if she had hoped he would cheer her up, and he didn't or if she just didn't want to be alone. He decided he was overthinking it. James walked into her bedroom and she was wrapped up tightly with a heating pad under her back and a sleeping mask over her eyes. James smiled and leaned over the bed and hugged her.

"I'll see you soon, ok?" She grumbled an acknowledgement and he left to drive the hour home.

GIFTS

A small gift is better than a great promise –
German Proverb

James talked to his daughter about her plans for after school. She was going to go to her mother's to eat. He asked her if she needed him for anything that night and asked for permission to be gone for the evening. She said it was cool, and that she was happy he had found someone to date.

"Date? I am not dating her. It's not like that. She just needed a friend and I did too. I mean if you are going to pick a friend, pick a really pretty one." His daughter laughed.

Now James had thought all the way home last night that Casey seemed very out of sorts and offered no real reason why. Now it did not seem to be him, or she would not have invited him over. So what had changed? Casey had been less angst filled and more personally social. Maybe it was George? He had taken the chairs from that little table.

Maybe that was it. She was rebuilding her life and that was a setback. Now James had three tables and didn't need them. But decided that he didn't want to give them away either.

James drove towards Wal-Mart not really sure what he wanted to do but knowing he needed groceries. Passing the pawn shop he decided to stop and see if they might have a French horn or movies. This was something he did about once a quarter anyway, and although he found a movie now and again he never found the French horn. Leaving the shop he noticed a consignment shop. It had always been there, but he had just never had a reason to go inside. But Casey needed chairs and they had several outside in the parking lot.

James walked over and looked at them and then went inside. They actually had nice second hand items. In the back buried like it had been there a while was a white dining room table and chairs. They even had a bread platter on top. James went over and looked at it and saw they wanted $150 for it. Now what did he want to do? He felt bad because he had already bought her socks and a cabinet and she seemed irritated by that. The cost was not a big deal really. Well it was money and he didn't have a lot of money. But to take someone out on a date on the town would easily cost a hundred dollars and they liked to stay home and talk. "It's a wash really," rationalized James. He offered the owner seventy five and they haggled to a hundred twenty.

James loaded it up and drove the hour to her house and set it up for her. She wouldn't be home for another two hours, so he went to the grocery store and bought some things for his house. James then went back to hers after she should have been home. She had not arrived yet. That was ok. He was just excited that he found something white and girlie to fill her dining room area up and give her some peace of mind back. He sat at the table and waited for her. When she arrived she looked at the table and him and looked irritated.

"Why are you here? I didn't ask you to come over." James was at loss. She was absolutely right. He had come over without being asked. She had given him a key? Had he presumed too much from that? He didn't take anything, he added something. A thousand ideas spun around his head. "What is this table?"

"Do you like it?" James was still trying to figure out how bad he had messed up coming over unannounced. "I thought you needed a place to sit when you eat. It looks nice, don't you think?"

She looked it over, "I don't think I would have picked it." James smiled. "But it was nice and unnecessary of you."

"I know. Story of my life – nice and unnecessary." James picked up his keys and cell phone as he slipped his feet into his shoes.

"Where are you going?"

"Home. Don't get the wrong impression I am not upset or anything. You are right, I should not have come without your telling me I had an open invitation. I'm sorry." She didn't disagree with him. She went into the kitchen and made a pot of coffee.

"You don't have to go." She didn't look at him. She moved around the kitchen mechanical.

"What's wrong Casey? You have not been acting the same the last two days? Did I upset you?"

"No." She looked at him with sad puppy dog eyes. "I'm sorry. I just hurt. My back hurts. I am not used to trying to dance like this in six inch heels and I don't like that place." James lost a hundred pounds instantly. He was not the source of her discomfort, and all he had had to do was ask. He should have done it sooner.

"You said being a dancer was going to be

temporary till you could find a job. Have you found anything?"

"That's where I was tonight. A customer was telling me about a job, and I went and had a drink with him, and he gave me his card." She looked in her purse and set it out on the table.

"Well that's good if leads to a job. But be careful. Not everyone has the right intentions."

She looked at him and smiled. "Not everyone comes over with a kitchen table."

James raised his eyebrows, "Um and chairs and ah, this bread bowl platter thingy. And the table has a drawer. See." James went into show-off-playful mode. Casey smiled for the first time in days. She sat at her new table and sorted out her pocket book. James sat across from her and watched her as she organized and they talked and talked. James could not have been happier. When she went to bed, he slept on the couch, but he set the timer on his phone and woke up very early and drove home in time to take his teenager to school. Then he went home and took a nap.

FOOD

"Lips however rosy, must be fed." - Unknown

James asked Casey every time he left if he could be here when she got home, when he was available to do so. Every time, Casey responded with a smile and a nod. James would arrive about an hour before each time and he would clean her apartment. She was not very tidy, not incredibly messy but still didn't clean up after herself; which was in contrast to personal hygiene, because Casey was ultraclean.

James would have a dinner idea and stop and get the necessaries, and he would have brought a movie should they want to do that. Casey had no possessions of her own that a person might consider a collection. No board games, no computer games, no Xbox or Playstation. Her radio didn't even pick up stations well, and her movie collection was less than eight titles. She didn't even have a TV. Actually, her not having a TV was one of the many things he thought they had in common. He hated TV but needed one to play his Xbox or his Wii and to entertain his children.

James began cooking and washed the dishes that somehow appeared in the sink. Preheating the oven, he immediately smelled something odd. Opening the oven he discovered a cookie sheet with a lump of coal on it. Now it wasn't coal in the beginning, maybe bruschetta? But apparently it had been cremated and not yet placed in an urn. She would later tell him she had forgotten she put it in the oven when she came home from work. Then she discovered it before she left for work the next day. "The oven was on all night?" James asked. Casey laughed like it was no big deal and even commented that she had done things similar before and for him not to worry. But James did worry and it motivated him to come more often and regular.

James enjoyed himself taking care of her. She was always so appreciative that he did so. Carol had always had to have everything her way and then would complain that he never did anything. But Casey would come home and see the house cleaner than she would have kept it, and she would tell James "Thank you." That crumb of appreciation was all it took for him to clean again the next time.

Visit after visit was becoming a routine for them. He would clean up and have dinner ready for her when she got home. He would take her coat and set her place at the table, then they would enjoy a meal together.

James had all the food groups necessary, including desert. And he always arranged it in some artsy attempt knowing that Casey was a fine arts major and once the domestic partner of a professional chef. James didn't really feel he had to compete with the long gone chef, but when Casey would compare his attempts of cooking to the chef's, most often in a degrading way. James would smile inside anyway. He might not be the professional chef, but he was eating dinner with Casey almost every night. "So he can have the praise and I will have the girl", thought James.

The next reward was even better. Casey would disrobe and go take a bath and demand that James sit beside the tub and talk to her. Outsiders might think that this naked beautiful woman aroused him and was the reason that James smiled sitting next to the tub. It was in a very small way, but in a very giant way was the fact that she trusted him. James did not touch her nor even look at her too much or too long. He brought her coffee, listened to her day, told her jokes and stories, and in the end gave her a bathrobe and privacy, while he set up the couch for a movie. It was a wonderful routine and James was starved for appreciation and attention. Casey gave him both.

James knew that too much of a good thing became a common place thing and would eventually be under-valued because of its regularity. He thought it might be time to mix it up a little.

"We always stay in. Let's go out to eat. I know a wonderful place. Ever been to a Brazilian Steak House?" Casey said no and James began to describe it to her. "It's like a buffet sort of. There is a table that you get your greens and salad and stuff; but what a waste that is because the real gem of a Brazilian Steak House is they have a parade of meat. All these waiters carry swords or skewers of meat and as they pass your table they offer you their goods. It is a man's dream come true! Right after sex of course."

"Well you better be happy you're gonna get as much meat as you want because you won't be getting any sex." They laughed. James had really not even thought about sex until now. They had talked about sex of course, but it was about what he had done in the Navy and she had done in college. It was not a taboo subject. It just didn't seem to be on their agenda.

Casey wore a white blouse and went with very little make up. She was a natural beauty, and her smile was so radiant it lit up the whole room. James watched her mouth as she talked. A couple of times he glanced down at her breasts and laughed at himself. After all, he had already seen them in all their glory. But here she was, a dozen years younger than him and far more beautiful than he deserved. And she was excited and loved to talk to him.

So did he want to have sex with her? Of course he did. He was a male after all and she was a very beautiful girl that had a flirty personality and sensual way about her. But he couldn't let himself go there. He valued her friendship far more than some romp in the hay; to lose her over a simple sexual desire when she had so much more to offer as a friend. He looked at her. She was exploring the room with her eyes. James recommended she look at the menu for the restaurant's specialties.

She had the specialty Brazil alcohol drink and cinnamon banana something. The whole experience was new to her, and he loved the feeling of being able to give it to her for the first time.

At the end of dinner he asked her would she go home for Thanksgiving. She said her sister and mom lived in town, but she didn't want to see them. "Well if you have nowhere planned to go, then would you come and be my guest for Thanksgiving? I always eat with my sister and then my friends. We don't have to cook anything but we usually do. You wouldn't need to of course. I will do that part. Last year my oldest daughter and I baked seven pies."

She didn't act as if she wanted to come but then she softened up and said, "If you want me to I will."

"Of course I do." James reached across the table and squeezed her hand.

THANKSGIVING

"We are having the usual things for Thanksgiving Dinner: Relatives." - Unknown

James was very excited. He had a date, sorta. Casey was coming to meet his friends. The Thanksgiving Dinner invite started right after his wife left him. His friends had been there for him. They always had been there in times of crisis. James well understood the idea that friends are the family you choose. Today he hoped that his family would grow by one. He was excited for many reasons. Casey was educated, and she was more age appropriate than his last romantic attempt. Casey was beautiful and most importantly they had a wonderful dynamic between them.

The socializing part was an hour before time to eat the Thanksgiving Dinner. James called Casey and asked where she was in the hour drive to get to him. She didn't answer. His first thought was she couldn't get to her phone fast enough because she was not the type of person to clutch the phone constantly and it wasn't readily available. She would call him in a minute.

Ten minutes later he called her again. This time when she didn't answer, he remembered the multiple occasions when she would look at who was calling and decide that it was too much anxiety to converse and just set the phone aside. James sent her a text asking her to call him as soon as possible.

All his kids were home, and they gathered up everything and drove away to dinner. There is an advantage to having older children. They are built in babysitters as long as you did not make it a chore, but an opportunity to negotiate in family and individual desires. Once situated it was like the previous two Thanksgivings, everyone was sitting and laughing and telling mostly old stories with a few new events weaved into the thread. The familiarity of it all made it feel like family even though three sets of families were represented.

James had been very excited about them meeting Casey. He knew she was wonderful and expected that they would think so too. An hour passed and she hadn't texted. James walked out on the deck and texted her again, "Are you ok?" He looked off the back deck into the tree line. The air was brisk but not too cold. His phone vibrated. Casey was calling.

"Hello?"

"Hi. I'm ok."

"I'm missing you. Are you on your way yet?"

"I can't come today. I'm sorry." Casey's voice was low and filled with anxiety.

James didn't want to make it harder than he knew it was for her. So he humored, "Ah, they don't bite, and the food hasn't killed me yet. I brought dessert so I know that's going to be good. The only thing missing is this wonderful friend that I want all my other friends to meet." There was considerable silence. James thought through all the possibilities and imagined her sitting on the edge of her bed with tear stained cheeks – alone.

"Casey, If you don't come I won't be angry with you. But you are wanted here. Everyone is excited about meeting the girl I talk so much about. And should it get overwhelming for you, although I can't see that happening, all you need do is take a hold of my forearm and I'll make an exit for us." Another long silence, James looked at his phone to see if was still connected.

"Casey, stand up honey. Find something nice and casual to wear. We are all in jeans and plain shirts. This isn't church, this is being thankful for good friends and having food and success in our lives. Forget everyone else that's here. I want you to know I am thankful that you are in my life. Come sit next to me and eat."

"I don't remember how to get to your house."

James smiled. He gave her directions again and offered to meet her half way. The offer sounded like him being a guide but it was really to make it time sensitive. She would be more motivated to getting there if she believed he was sitting beside the road waiting for her. He did not put her in overdrive however. He would wait a long time.

While thanksgiving festivities were going on, James sat in the parking lot of a little convenience store in a town so small it had two stops lights, one on either end of town. James thought the only reason for them was to make people stop and have to see the elaborate Welcome To signs that the town had at these intersections.

It was a half hour to get there and he had been waiting twenty minutes. The smell of food was still in his brain if not his nostrils. He felt hungry. James called Casey. She told him where she was, and she said she had left but he could tell in his gut she hadn't. So he told her how cold it was in his car waiting for her and that he was going to go get some hot chocolate from the little store and that she should look for him to the right after the light.

The store was out of hot chocolate. James got a large coffee and they had a basket of sausage biscuits. He thought about refraining but he loved food and really loved sausage. So he picked up the biscuit and walked back outside. Pacing around the van he ate his biscuit and drank the coffee. It didn't taste very good. Not quite horrible Navy coffee, but definitely not the premium roast that Casey loved and made.

His coffee was cold and nearly empty. James hated to waste food, it was his rationale for over eating and it prevented the purchase of Tupperware. But this time the coffee was not going to cut it. He took the top off and poured it on the ground. James walked over and threw his cup in the trash can and then pulled out his phone. It had been well over forty-five minutes to drive twenty five. He wondered should he go get her, that would have been quicker had he done that from the beginning. He wondered should he just leave knowing Casey wasn't going to show. But he didn't know that. If she was to show up, and he wasn't there, then she really would be anxiety ridden. He had watched her zombie out enough that he didn't want Casey to spend her Thanksgiving like that.

She answered on the first ring, "I don't see a town?"

James was awash with thought. She was driving. She was attentive and she had answered on the first ring. She was coming. He had almost given up on that idea. "What do you see?"

"Um, farmlands and wait some houses up there and a stop light."

James walked out to the street and looked south. "I see you. Drive up here." She pulled in the parking lot and rolled down the window. James brushed her hair behind her ear to expose her face. "Thanks for coming. Just follow me there. Ok?" She didn't smile but nodded.

James turned around and belched, "excuse me." He rubbed his stomach and grinned half embarrassed. Then climbed into his van and lead her to Thanksgiving dinner.

The front lawn was a parking lot and although they had a long walk down the driveway, they would not have to ask anyone to move so they could leave. Everything in life is a trade-off. Stay positive and find the good in any situation.

Casey got out of her car and walked over to him. She looked scared and sad. She was not the bright eyed person that he spent all his time with recently. She was still beautiful, but there was something just below the surface. She was terrified and

James could see it. How could a stripper, even a reluctant one, be afraid of a thanksgiving dinner? James walked over and took her hand in his. Squeezing it, James led Casey to the house a few steps and then let her go.

Everyone kept doing their own thing. As they passed Casey, each one introduced themselves and made comments about James and how he was part of the collective family. That means they couldn't get rid of him. "Like a bad penny," one friend commented. Casey seemed very nervous. She didn't talk to anyone and scowled most of the time. James noticed, but he was having other concerns. Something in his stomach was at war.

James slipped out the back door and walked to the tree line behind the cars. He bent over and vomited violently. There wasn't much in his stomach but that nasty gas station coffee and sausage biscuit. He purged again and again, but then he felt better. Returning to the house, he made his way to the bathroom and washed his face. He looked tired in the mirror, but he realized that Casey had been alone for at least 15 minutes, an eternity of someone who has panic attacks. Walking out, he was happy to see that his boisterous friend had taken to talking to her even if he was fishing for information. She was a fortress and James came over and wrapped his arm around her arm and led her away to the deck.

His eldest daughter was standing outside. He was happy to see her. She had been attending her first year of college. James missed her immensely. She offered to take a picture of James and Casey, and James asked Casey if it would be ok. She nodded and stood close to him although she didn't look like her heart was in it. James eldest daughter smiled, "One more, in case that one doesn't come out well."

James led her to the dinner table but as he pulled her chair out his stomach went back to war with the rest of his body. He leaned over and whispered to Casey, "I'll be right back." Then he went to the bathroom and fought back the nausea.

Sitting at the table the hostess tried to fill his plate but he kept refusing one item after another. "Are you ok? Not the James that I know to refuse food."

"Honestly, I am not feeling so well suddenly." He looked over at Casey and decided that he had to try to keep it together. She had overcome so much anxiety to come have dinner. He wasn't about to let her down now. But somewhere in the next ten minutes it was obvious that this wasn't going to end well. Looking at Casey, James reached out and took her hand. "I think I might need to go home prematurely." Casey nodded and slid her plate aside.

"No honey. You can stay if you want, or you can go home. I'll even invite you to stay with me in the guest room, but I won't be very good company I am afraid."

"I'll go home with you." Casey took his hand and squeezed it. They stood up and James apologized to everyone and then asked his older children to take the little ones home. Everything in order, Casey followed him home.

That day and night was very long. James ran to the toilet over and over again. Things did not care from which end they erupted. The hours went by as a painful blur. Casey was there the whole time. He was happy she was there, but sad he could not enjoy her company.

The next morning he awoke at day break. Casey was lying in his bed with him. Her head rested on his hip. It was then he realized that she had taken care of him all night. She had brought him glasses of water and hot wash cloths. She had wiped the sweat from his chest and cleaned his bathroom each time.

The girl he had tried so hard to be a friend to had returned the attention at his absolute worst. She had taken care of him. James could not remember the last time anyone cared for him so attentively, except for his granny when he was a boy.

Then James realized she was here with him. The start of his day included her. His whole body was weak, but suddenly it filled with a tingle and warmth. He dared not move because he was afraid she would wake up and want to leave. But nature called and he gently slid away.

When he returned, Casey had ascended the bed and laid her head on the pillows. "Do you feel better?" she asked.

"Much. Thank you for staying. That was very nice of you."

Casey smiled warmly and he lay down next to her and she patted his chest. She rolled over to him and laid her face against his skin. His heart pounded. James knew right then he was in trouble. His heart was going to jump out of his chest.

They slept awhile more, and then Casey got up and made breakfast.

James was feeling a lot better which only made him certain it was food poisoning. But the thing he couldn't stop thinking about was the beautiful woman that couldn't really take care of herself had just spent the night taking care of him. No one had been that loving or doting over him since his granny over twenty years ago.

The next couple of days James prepared to spoil his children for their birthday. Being around Thanksgiving and just before the Christmas shopping surge, people were seldom willing to attend birthday parties. James had cakes and made the affairs small and filled with family. As he looked at his family he felt warm and happy but at the same time something was missing. A light had come into his life. He had gone into the darkness of another person's world and within it had found hope.

Casey did not do well in crowds. But she

held it together at Thanksgiving. She had nursed him all night with caring hands and affection. She had no children of her own and didn't seem to want make any. But she loved kids and liked playing with them. James wished she was with them now, laughing and eating cake.

James and Casey were not really dating. They didn't hold hands. They didn't kiss at the end of the night. They were just two people who needed someone to believe in them. James wanted someone to think he was important and be willing to let him spoil them. Casey was a person that felt abused by the world and wanted someone to think she was worth being spoiled.

They were a good match. She was so deprived of love and affection that every drop he showed was received like a flood. When James' wife had left after his illness, he had fantasized that should he ever commit to another woman that he hoped she had been in a bad relationship where she wasn't appreciated so that being with him she would feel the power of a positive influence. Casey seemed to be this person.

James was not really sure about this. Casey had some real issues that he wasn't confident he understood. But what he did know was that she had treated him better when he was sick than his wife of twenty years had ever done at any time. He wanted to scoop her up and hug her and kiss her and tell her thank you but he knew if he did these physical things she might think he wanted more. Well he did want more. He wanted to kiss her. He wanted to hold her hand. He wanted to grab her and dance in the kitchen. He wanted her to know she was important to him and that he wanted her in his life. But James was afraid. Not that he wasn't a good man and worth having but that he was twelve years older than her. Casey had so many bad experiences that she might not be receptive to dating if it could possibly lead to rejection and more disappointment.

James knew he had come to love every second of sharing life with Casey, a feeling that he had never known before. If he put his heart out there, she might run and he would lose her. If he were too patient, Casey might think him not interested and someone else might sneak in and tell her she was more important. "Dammit" he thought. "Risk it all and tell her that I love her."

Casey had stayed all Thanksgiving weekend, but it was Sunday and time for her to go home. Standing in the kitchen, she had placed her stuff on the table and was chatting about something but his mind was elsewhere.

James walked over and took her hands and turned her to face him. "Casey, ", James took a deep breath, "I want to ask permission to date you. Would you be willing to be my girlfriend?"

Casey didn't smile. James heart sank. She looked at him and then looked out the big picture window. James felt a tremble in his chest. Casey squeezed his hands and James prepared himself for the worse. She looked back at him and a smile crept across her face. Casey leaned in and lifted herself on her toes and kissed him lightly on the lips. "Yes, I would like that."

James heart started to beat so fast it could have exploded. Casey set her keys on the table and then wrapped her arms around him and he pulled her tightly into a long hug. "You have made me a very happy man. I hope I can make you a very happy woman."

"You already have," she said. "You already have."

Casey left and went home. They texted a few times, and he promised to come see her after work the next day.

James was the president of the PTA. He would often wonder what people would think of him if they knew he was dating a stripper. Didn't really matter what they thought. Casey made him very happy. He had spent four years of his life leading fund raisers and giving his time effort and often his own money to better his kid's school. On rare occasions people would say thank you, but it wasn't very often. He found himself at the school helping with some last minute details of a fund raiser.

One of his children's teachers was standing in the hall, and she commented that James was wearing a large smile. "I have a lot to smile about today. I have a girlfriend for the first time since being divorced, and she makes me very happy."

The teacher beamed, "Good for you. I remember when Jonathon asked me to be his girlfriend. We had just ended our second date, and he looked at me and said I was terrific and wonderful. Then he told me that if I were going to be around all the time I had to meet his son. That if I didn't like his kids, then it wouldn't work out, but he was sure that his son and I would get along famously. He was right." James had done a lot to hide

Casey from his girls. Not because she was bad, but because they always seemed to think that a boy and a girl had to be dating. James had been afraid they would scare Casey off, but now they would be dating. And the teacher was right. If the relationship was going to work, it had to include the children in some capacity.

You couldn't scrub that smile from his face, but his brain was spinning out of control on how to introduce Casey to his younger children. They had met briefly at the Thanksgiving dinner but had not interacted at all. He needed a way for them all to be able to interact.

James was ready to dedicate himself to her, but she would have to get the approval of the most important people in his life – his kids. And so that first weekend of December he had his visitation. So He planned a double birthday surprise to take them all to Great Wolf Lodge and the indoor water park.

James discussed the details with Casey

and smiled when he told her his objective. "Casey, I want you to come so that my kids first meeting with you is a joyful fun one. If we are going to date, then they need to see that you have a wonderful personality, are friendly and happy. Oh and one last thing, you have to like them, but they have love you." James hugged Casey and smiled at her. "No pressure." He could see in her eyes that she was already terrified. Just over thirty never married, no kids, and no experience, being a role model for young people was not the job she had in mind. But she decided that it was a good idea and agreed to go.

December 2010

"You can do anything with children if you only play with them" – German Proverb.

James called the lodge and rented a two bedroom suite. There were two twin beds in one room and a king size bed in the other. James thought about how it might look for him to be staying in a bedroom with a woman they didn't know. The little two were very young and wouldn't have any idea of what would be happening in that room. In fact, James had no idea what would be happening in that room.

Casey had begun kissing him but they were not long deep passionate kisses. They were quick lip kisses to show affection and move on with tasks at hand. He didn't mind really. He was just happy that she wanted to kiss him at all.

James invited his second daughter's best friend and made her keep it a secret. All the plans came together and that Friday he picked everyone up and announced where they were going and why. His three girls in attendance (a fourth was at college) and his oldest daughter's friend were excited and ready for an indoor water park in December.

The adventure became exciting right away. Before they could even get out of town, blue lights were flashing, and he was being pulled over.

The highway patrol officer walked up to the window, and James inquired to the trouble.

"As I past you I noticed you weren't wearing a seat belt," alleged the trooper.

"Well, I have to disagree. I am sure you may have looked but I am afraid you were mistaken. I always wear my seat belt. I did even before it was a law. Not to mention that I have a van full of kids, and what kind of example would I be if I didn't make everyone buckle up." The trooper looked in the van and saw the scared faces of all the girls.

The trooper took James' license and registration and then walked back to his car.

"Well this is inconvenient" James snickered.

"Daddy, you had your seat belt on!"

"I know honey, but there is no reason to argue with him. He will have to decide if what he saw was accurate, and if he does then we will just have to argue over it in court. No need to get stressed out over it and let it ruin our awesome weekend." The girls didn't look scared anymore. They looked angry. "Hey, who is going to go water sliding this weekend?"

"Me!" they all yelled in unison and then started a chatter of laughter and joking and aspirations to which slide and how many times. The laughter poured from the van as the trooper walked up. When he placed his face in the window, they all stopped laughing and scowled at him.

"Here you go. Sorry to have bothered

your family. Keep those seatbelts on." Then he turned and walked away.

"See girls. It is easier to stay out of trouble than it is to get out of trouble. Always wear your seatbelt and be polite to people."

It was an hour's drive to Casey's house, but it was mostly on the way. When he was about fifteen minutes away, he called her and she didn't answer, Thanksgiving all over again. James bit his lip, but didn't show his anxiety to the kids.

He pulled into her apartment complex, and the kids were excited because it had started to snow. She had not answered the phone but he didn't want to alarm the girls. "Ok, everyone. Stay in the van, I am going to leave it running with the heater on. Jamie, Honey, come sit in the front seat and make sure no one tries to drive away."

James' disability had left him with severe balance issues as well as significant hearing loss. This was the first real test of his balance, and he wasn't doing exceptionally well on the slippery surface. But he managed to make it up to her third floor apartment.

He knocked on the door as he was letting himself in. Casey was sitting at the kitchen table, her phone was lain out in front of her. "Come on honey, let's go."

"I'm not going." She looked frozen in fear as if she had been crying recently but not currently.

"Casey, we don't have time today for a long discussion, and how it's all going to be ok. I know they are little monsters, but they are my loveable little monsters and they are going to love you. Did you pack?" Casey nodded her head and James went into bedroom and got the two bags by the bed. Walking through the living room he smiled at her, "It's going to be ok. They are going to love you. Get your things together and let's go."

Now James thought it was difficult

walking around in the snow on his own and now he was carrying two suitcases. He had to stop and set them down twice to gather his senses and fight off the nausea. He thought about his Aunt. She had lupus from her early twenties and became more and more crippled over the years. She would tell him that she wasn't disabled she was impaired. She could do anything she wanted, but she just had to find new ways of doing things. She was James hero, now so more than ever. He wished she was still alive so he could tell her.

Putting Casey's bags in the back of the van, James' youngest, Cindy, asked "Where is your girlfriend?"

"She's getting ready. I'll be honest she looks like she is scared to death. So when she gets here just keep being yourselves and try not to ask a million questions. Play Mad Libs or something. We have all weekend to get to know each other."

James went back up the stairs, and Casey

was still sitting at the table. He put her phone in her pocket book and then her keys. He leaned over and kissed her on top of the head. "Did you get toothbrushes and things?"

"They are in my bag."

"Well then, we are ready to go."

"I'm not going."

"And why not?"

"I can't."

"You can't or you don't want to?"

"I can't." her face twisted and she began to cry. James stood next to her and wrapped his arms around her and hugged her tightly.

"They are excited about meeting you. Of course they are more excited about the water slides and Magic Quest, but at least you are in the top three." That didn't help; she squeezed him harder and continued to cry. "Casey, Honey, they want to spend the weekend with you. They want to meet the girl that makes their daddy so happy. They already know all the best things about you, because I have told them. Now it's just time for you to meet them." James took her hands and lifted her to a standing position. "Now go clean up your face and I'll be back in two minutes to get you. Go." He patted her on the bottom (which was the first time) and she looked at him as if she were put off.

James slipped and slide back to the Van. "Sorry kids for the delay but she really is scared of meeting you guys."

The youngest, Cindy, smiled a little cherub grin and said, "She's afraid of me." Then batted her eyelashes. It reminded James of a bad horror film opening.

Snickering, "Yeah, you little devil and I am too now." James reached in and tussled her hair and blew her a kiss. She loved her daddy, and she ate up the attention. As James turned to get Casey, he saw her coming down the stairs with yet another bag. That made three. He thought to remark that it was just a two day trip but decided not to cause her any more anxiety. She had after all made it out of the apartment. It only took her twenty minutes.

Great Wolf lodge was another 3 hours away, but the trip went by fast with all the conversation and singing and playing Mad Libs. James kept glancing over at Casey. She had this look of amazement and disbelief on her face as if she had never experienced this type of family interaction. Casey was quiet and distant, so James reached over and squeezed her thigh. She placed her hand over his and wrapped her fingers tightly though his fingers. Looking at her he smiled and she looked at him with a tight blank expression that slowly relaxed and then she returned the smile. It was painted with uncertainty.

They checked into the lodge and the girls squealed with excitement as they explored the spacious accommodations. James put all the suitcases in the appropriate rooms.

Placing the bags in the master bedroom he glanced at the large bathtub. That would fit two he thought, but he didn't want to presume too much.

Casey walked in and looked at the tub. "I am going to take a bubble bath in that." She nodded determined and affirmative. James smiled wide; it was the first time she looked like she might be having fun. "I was wondering would you mind if we went to the ABC store and bought some bourbon?"

James kept being amazed. Bourbon was his favorite spirit. Casey just kept being his perfect match. And if she wanted Bourbon then he would find some but it made him a little sad. Casey noticed this and asked, "Why the face?"

"What? What face?"

Casey took his hand, "You looked worried." He was worried. If she were going to be romantic with him, he wanted it to be sober so he would know that she was choosing uninhibited to be with him.

James forced a grin, "I was just thinking I didn't have any idea where a liquor store might be. Plus, I have never seen you drink except for the time at the Brazilian steak house. "

"Is it ok if I have a drink?" Casey asked.

"Of course it is. You are a grown woman. I drink. Not only that I usually only drink Bourbon or tequila. So again, you seem to be a perfect match for me." Casey wrinkled her nose as if she didn't share his belief. James had Jamie commit to watching the family. She had just turned sixteen and her best friend was nineteen, so the two of them should have been able to handle the task. James and Casey went back to the van and found a store pretty close to the lodge. Purchasing a bottle of *Elijah Craig* they headed back to the lodge.

Entering the bedroom, Casey remarked that they had nothing to mix the bourbon with. "Mix?" James seemed disgusted. "I just pour it over ice."

"Well get some ice, but I'd like some sprite or *Coke* or something, but not *Pepsi*." James acknowledged that he didn't like *Pepsi* with or without alcohol in it. He went off into the maze of hallways looking for an ice machine and a vending machine. When he returned to the suite, the girls had already bathed and put on their pajamas. He told the older girls to hang out in the living room and rent a movie if they wanted to. Then he went in the bedroom and kissed his little ones good night. They were very excited about the next day. They had wanted to do the day spa, but that seemed very expensive considering he had five girls with him. He struck that down fast and furious.

Walking through the living area, he paused and kissed both Jamie and her friend on the top of their heads and then went to his own room. When he walked inside the first thing he noticed was that Casey's clothes were folded on the end of the bed. He looked at the bathroom door and it was wide open. He couldn't see the tub but he could hear her in it.

James sat down on the end of his bed and remembered another time when this happened. Twenty three years ago, he had met a beautiful woman. She was on vacation, and after three days of spending time with him, they ended up at his apartment and she was taking a shower and she left the door cracked open. He was twenty then. He sat on his bed and wondered if she was inviting him in by not shutting the door. He sat there forever worried and panic filled. Now twenty three years later nothing had changed. He was a school boy scared to death. He had four kids and an ex-wife and been very promiscuous before his marriage. But somehow he was intimidated, frightened that everything was about to change. He took a big breath and decided that he had already seen Casey naked, although before he had no desires. "Maybe I'll just brush my teeth and not look." So he walked into the bathroom and picked up his toothbrush. Looking over he saw that the Elijah Craig had not been opened. He walked out and filled two plastic cups with ice and Coke and then went to the bathroom and poured a drink for each of them.

"That is really going to suck when you drink it with tooth paste mouth, dummy." James turned and looked at her. She was covered in bubbles and nothing was showing but her beautiful face. She was right too, bourbon and Colgate not a good combination. Laughing he placed her glass on the edge of the tub and she lifted her body up and out of the protective bubbles. Her large breasts floated as the bubbles raced off the sides. His heart started pounding. This was turning into a relationship that he wasn't sure he was ready for.

He looked her in the eyes. "Is there room in there for me?"

She smiled coy, "Yep, but this is my

bath. You can't come in."

"Really? Such a tease." She smiled beaming at him.

"Sit beside the tub and talk to me." So he did. They talked until the water was cold. She laughed and commented that she had really enjoyed the ride here. He commented that she didn't look like she enjoyed it. "I didn't think I was ready." She took a third sip from the glass of Bourbon and it was still mostly full and watery now. "Go get me that robe on the bed."

James went out and brought her the robe. He laid it across the toilet and then went into the other room and took his clothes off, except his briefs. He was trying to decide if he wanted to push his luck or be patient. Did she want him to be assertive or sensitive? Considering he had been mostly sensitive and only guiding in his assertiveness, he decide to keep a little barrier between them. Standing up, he looked in the mirror and then he realized that she was about to see him naked for the first time. He was fat and twelve years older and disabled and poor. Why was she here with him? He felt a pain of inadequacy and fear rushed over him, and James began to sweat. Just at that moment she appeared in the doorway wrapped up in her white fluffy robe.

When she saw him standing there in his under-ware she smiled. "Don't get too excited there big boy. You aren't going to fuck me." That was a relief. It wouldn't have lasted very long anyway; it had been way too long since the last time. But on an upside she had given him the look over and was not put off in any noticeable way. In fact, her eyes looked filled with soft tenderness. She walked over and ran her nails across his chest. Fire burned across his conscious. He became instantly aroused. She lay down across the bed and then untied her robe. James sat down next to her and slowly he reached over and opened the cloth so he could see all of her.

As he studied her gentle form, his eyes met hers. "Do you prefer younger women?" she asked.

"I prefer intelligent women that carry themselves well and are creative. You seem too good to be true."

A smile adorned her face and she reached out and squeezed his forearm. "Lick me."

James eyebrow wrinkled. It had been many, many years. His arousal disappeared as anxiety filled him. She squeezed his arm again. "Lick me now." So he did. She scratched his head, arched her back, and made little noises that just filled him with joy. And when her thighs began to jerk and tremble, she pulled herself away and threw her head on the pillow.

He watched her. She didn't say thank you. She didn't say I love you. She didn't give him anything in return. But what did he want? He smiled. James wanted far less than she had given him. Selfish as she seemed, spoiling her like this was a wonderful feeling.

No one woke up early. The little ones finally turned on cartoons around nine thirty. James woke up and could smell her perfume. He looked over at her in his bed. She was beautiful, and she was lying naked next to him. With all her anxiety, he was happy that she felt safe and appreciated by him. He had not felt appreciated for nearly all of his marriage. How had he suddenly become so fortunate?

He went out and motivated the crowd to get dressed and ready for a buffet breakfast. Casey came out of the bedroom ready first. James was amazed, that was highly unexpected. She smiled at him and said, "I am not a friendly person until I have had my coffee." James nodded and smiled.

He herded his group down to the buffet area, and they all enjoyed breakfast. Planning a strategy for the day it of course included a mad rush for the indoor water park. So they headed back to the room and suited up. Casey was wearing a turquoise bikini that came with a wrap. She was stunning. James still could not believe how lucky he was to have her in his life. The younger girls fought over her. Each wanted their Casey time where she only played with one of them exclusively. Casey seemed a little overwhelmed by all the attention but she tried to play with them equally until she was exhausted. Then she retired to the lounge chairs. I suppose you could lay out but James wasn't certain what the point would be. They were inside a building that had snow on the outside!

After fun pool time, Casey wandered off to go shopping. James and the girls discovered the long water slides. They waited in line and rode over and over again and then they all went to the wave pool. Casey returned and joined them. So they had to start over and do the long water slides again. It was a long exhausting and fun filled day. As the dinner time snuck up on them, they all went to the room and took baths and dressed for dinner.

Casey went and jumped in the shower and James braved up and jumped in with her. She looked at him like she was surprised he had come in without asking but he looked at her sternly and told her to turn around. She raised an eyebrow but did as she was told. James took a handful of her wet hair and lathered it up with shampoo. Then with a luffa, he scrubbed her whole body chin to toes. When he was done he kissed her and then handed her the luffa and turned around, "Back please." Casey scrubbed his back legs and soles of his feet.

They dried off and dressed for dinner, and then took his gaggle of girls down to the dining hall. The food at breakfast had been good, but dinner was a disappointment. Getting a six and eight year old to eat was hard enough, but when the food was bad, it was near impossible.

After dinner they went and played

Magic Quest, an electronic scavenger hunt that required special wands. Casey and Cindy went to an arcade and wound up clothing and jewelry shopping. This would become a bonding trend for them, two girls doing girlie things.

Everyone ran around and played. James got Daddy daughter time with number three, Shauna. Around ten everyone was completely exhausted. The crowd retreated to the bedrooms, and they were all tucked in.

James went into the bedroom, stripped down, brushed his teeth and went to bed. Casey snuggled up beside him and laid her head on his shoulder. Her warm body felt like heaven against his own. "Thank you for bringing me," she whispered and then ran her fingernails along his side making him squirm. James smiled, she did not often say thank you. He imagined it must have been a very good day.

Sleepovers

"Fear is not an unknown emotion to us." – Neil Armstrong.

The trip home was uneventful, and James spent more and more time at Casey's home and she at his. He sat down with Jamie and asked her if it was ok. "Yes Dad. I am good with it. I am so happy you found someone you like."

"I think it is more than just a like. I think I might try and keep this one."

Jamie smiled and hugged her dad. She was very outspoken and defended herself with great ferocity. Since she was very little, he could tell that she would be a leader. Anytime she walked into a room, even at age four, she would spend a few minutes evaluating everyone before joining in the play. By days end she would be the queen bee. Now that she was sixteen, it was no different.

But something was wrong. Carol had

already berated him saying that Jamie was complaining that he was never there and that she felt alone and isolated. James started making note of how he was behaving in front of his daughter. The reason he left at 5pm each day was because Jamie had already come and gone for the night, much like he had done when he was sixteen. He trusted her and she had her own car and an allowance, he didn't understand why she would be telling Carol that he wasn't home when neither was she. James made sure he was always there when she woke up and that he talked to her before school and that he engaged her after school before she ran off to do what free range sixteen year olds do. But something was still wrong.

James and Jamie sat down and discussed her therapy concerning being gay. Jamie wanted to be identified as a boy. James didn't know exactly what she meant by that so he asked her to explain with questions all along the way. The conversation did not go well. It was civil, but it was not received with the logic James thought it needed.

If Jamie were going to be a "boy", and she felt as if she were a boy trapped in a girl's body, then James explained that some of her lifestyle had to change as well. There could be no more sleepovers with her girlfriends in her room, nor visits behind closed doors. He explained that her sister brought boys home all the time, and that no boy ever made it past the living room / kitchen; thus if she were going to be interested in girls in a romantic way, then the visits she had enjoyed for years would be redefined. Jamie thought she was being treated unfairly. James told her that he loved her and was trying to understand, but that if she thought that he was treating her badly because he wouldn't give her opportunity to have sex then she was in for a much larger shock when she saw how society as a whole treated gay people. Jamie's attitude would get worse.

James shared the encounter with

Casey, and she commented that she once considered what it might be like to be with a girl when she was in college. James asked did she? Casey said no but she did think about it. Then Casey explained that teenage girls didn't know what they wanted and hormones all over the place. James commented that grown women didn't know what they wanted and hormones all over the place. Casey conceded that he may be right.

The following weekend they stayed at his house. She came over Friday after work and brought clothes to last the weekend. James drove back and forth every day, a hundred miles. He liked the idea that she had come to stay. The weekend was just normal. Jamie had decided to go sleep over with a friend and that left Casey and James the whole house to themselves. She had decided to be his girlfriend ten days ago. And although they had spent eight of those ten days together, they had no other encounter since the first night at Great Wolf Lodge.

James could have waited forever. He had that kind of patience but when she started flirting and teasing, he felt that sexual urge. Although he was worried because it had been so long, he was ready to make love to the woman that had captured his heart. Wrestling, tickling (which she hated) and finally stripping her naked, the games came to a screeching halt.

"You can't fuck me."

"What?" James thought, 'yes, I can.' And then he laughed to himself.

She got angry when he snickered, "I mean it. You can't fuck me."

"Well if you aren't ready that's fine. We don't have to rush." James ran his hand down her thighs and smiled at her. Leaning in he kissed her bellybutton.

"I mean it, stop."

"What's wrong, honey?"

She looked like she was starting a

panic attack. "If I let you fuck me, then you won't want me anymore, and you will just throw me away."

He blinked in disbelief. "Wow. Just wow." James rolled back and sat on his heels. "Do you really think that little of me? That everything I have done over the last month and a half was just to fuck you and then throw you away?" Casey looked genuinely concerned that that was the situation. "Honey, I don't know who hurt you so badly. But you have placed me in a very awkward position. If I keep wanting I look like a dick and if I don't, then I look like I don't want you. I can't win in either scenario." James stood up and gathered up all the clothes. To make time pass, he folded them and sat them at the end of the couch. He looked over at her with a great sadness on his face. Reaching out he scooped up her head and pulled her close to him. Leaning down he kissed her cheek. "I love you, Casey. I am not going to push you, and I'm definitely not going to throw you away. I just need to go think. I am not angry, but I just don't know what to say." James walked into the bedroom and lay across his bed. Had he pushed her too hard too fast? This was six weeks, and they were adults.

He had known other girls that couldn't wait two hours after they met him, and she was nervous after six weeks. It was really up to her though. Last night she had stripped off her pants and teased him with her nakedness but not offered to share. And today, she threw up a wall. As he pondered all the possibilities, he realized twenty minutes had passed then he heard her in the kitchen. She walked into the bedroom, naked as the day she was born.

She walked beside him lying on the bed and pressed her lady against the side of his head. "Do you want to fuck me?"

James rolled over and looked up at her. "No. I want to make to love to you - today, tomorrow, always. But don't do it because you think it is what I want. Do it because you want to share with me and love me back. You don't owe me anything."

She looked sad, but she smiled and then she slid herself across his body and tugged and pulled at him until they aligned. Sinking herself over him, he took her in his arms and although inside her he hugged her more than having sex. They stayed in bed two hours taking short breaks before exploring one another again and again.

Sunday came, and she poked him around ten in the morning. He opened one eye and smiled. He felt stupid having the same thought every day, 'how lucky am I.' But then he would beam with joy. She smiled at him and looked like she was going to kiss him and then she whispered, "Make me some coffee." James chuckled, not the words he thought he was going to hear. She had made him a very very happy man yesterday and into the night. James got up and made her coffee.

I would like for you to come to lunch

with me today and meet my grandfather. His birthday was three days ago. He is a big time womanizer but in a very stoic way. Don't think he doesn't like you just because he doesn't smile or talk. And if you want to make his week, then after lunch just go up to him and hug him tight. With boobies like yours, he will wonder if his plumbing still works and then be disappointed to discover it doesn't.

"That's mean!"

"No, just true. He had to have his prostate removed. Not much going on any more. He complains occasionally, but granny's been gone a long time. My grandfather is the sweetest man in the world."

"I am going to have to disagree. My grandfather is the coolest. He loves me too. Spoils me rotten every time I see him." Casey beamed with pride.

"When did you see him last?"

"Not this summer but last summer. We went to Florida and rode around on his boat and went to bars. His old ass friends kept hitting on me."

"Florida? I love Florida. As soon as the girls are a little older, I am high tailing it down there. I hate this little town."

"You would love where he lives. We skirted little islands and just had a blast." This was the first time Casey had ever bragged about a life experience. James dared not interrupt and let her spin her tale of drinking with her grandfather and all of his stories. She began to explain that he was an entrepreneur and a pilot. She told of how he would fly them around and always have candies to pass out to them as children. You could see the warm admiration in her eyes. She had a genuine love, and her face shown like the sun as she shared her stories with James.

As time neared, James coaxed her into getting ready, and she was only about ten minutes late which wasn't too bad considering he planned for her to be five minutes over any way. They got to the restaurant at the same time as James' Papa. The elder man looked at his grandson and said, "Hello Mr. Knobbs."

James smiled at his Papa, "Good Day, Mr. Knobbs. I would like you to meet my girlfriend. May I introduce Casey. Casey this is my grandfather, James."

Papa looked at Casey and without cracking a grin informed her, "They named me after him." James had heard that lie a hundred times, but it still seemed pleasant to hear. Casey wrinkled her nose as if they were both odd, perhaps they were.

Casey looked around at the old country restaurant and did not look overly approving. But it was Papa's favorite and he wasn't going to change 60 years of habit for James' new girl- friend.

James wondered if he would give

Casey a chance. Papa really loved his ex-wife. Perhaps too much. And when things fell apart, he wanted to side with her but was torn between family and being the womanizer that he was. James tried to forgive him, but mostly he just ignored it since weighed against all Papa's virtues this one vice was easy to let slide. After all, she had been his granddaughter in law for twenty years too.

James filled in all the gaps by asking Papa questions and prompting him to tell stories. Casey looked perplexed as if she were plotting her escape route. But in the end she held it together and made a very good impression. James was pleased.

Soon after they got home, Casey informed him she was going to leave soon because she needed to get things done for work tomorrow. Now James didn't really know what that meant, but he decided that she had been exposed to enough for one weekend. He could tell she was still angst ridden, and all this family time and new love was causing anxiety. But it seemed to be a better kind of stress. He realized she hadn't been a zombie for quite some time.

Walls Start Falling Down

"To be trusted is a greater compliment than to be loved." – George Macdonald

That week James stayed over-night at Casey's apartment Tuesday night because Jamie went to visit her mother and said she didn't mind. Casey seemed very happy to have him there. But when she left for work, James was bored to tears. He left and went to the grocery store, locking the door this time. He bought a book to read and some groceries for dinner. When Casey got home he had made her a nice sit down meal.

"You didn't have to do all that," she remarked, but he could tell she was appreciative. She dug in and ate well. James liked making her happy. She was opening up more and more, telling him about her life. But she seemed to be holding a lot back, as if she had to think and decide what parts to reveal rather than just gush out all the details.

Casey was proud of her being in the high school band and band camps. She was sad about how her college love had abused her, and someone else took her dog. They discussed a rescue plan for her dog. She described him as a designer dog that was very intelligent and that she had trained him very well.

James had a dog, several over his life. None of them were particularly well trained. Casey talked about her dog as if he were a child, her child. And by the time she was done, she seemed sad and distant.

Casey got up and walked into her bedroom. James followed her. She took some pain medications off her sink and took them. Then she asked him to make her some coffee. James went in the kitchen and started the brew. Coffee at ten at night seemed a little late, but she also didn't have to get up before ten in the morning.

James walked in the bathroom, and she was soaking in the tub. "Are we going to watch a movie?" he asked.

"Wouldn't you rather watch me?"

"Depends, am I going to be invited in the tub?"

"Nope. But you can sit on the floor and talk to me." James did just that. They talked and talked. Listening to her stories and her listening to his was this concert of experiences played by a symphony that seemed to have rehearsed together forever. The stories flowed out like music and their eyes danced together while they shared.

"My brother invited me to hear my nephew sing this weekend. Would you like to come with me and the girls to hear it? I would love for you to meet my brother and mother."

"Why do you want me to meet everyone?"

"I want them to meet the woman that makes me so happy. You don't have to go, but I would love for you to join me."

"I'll go." She didn't sound enthusiastic but she didn't sound dread filled either. Perhaps she was warming up to the idea of a family.

"Will you be spending Christmas with your family? You know I am going to ask you to spend time with me and mine."

Casey moved the bubbles around and then looked over at him. "I don't get along with them, my family. They consider me the black sheep of our family."

James could not tell if there was anger in her voice or just apathy. "My family doesn't really talk much either. I don't avoid them, but they also don't insert themselves in my life in any way. In fact to have an extended family I have to do the work of inviting or visiting. Doesn't mean they don't love me, just that we aren't very tight."

"My family is disappointed in me. My Aunt in Charlotte threw me out of her house for being a bad example to her son, my cousin. It was all over a bottle of bourbon, but I was old enough, and I didn't give him any. But she was this selfish elite Christian zealot; always bossing the family around and my grandfather too. She is all in his affairs. I'll bet when he dies she will have everything in her name so she can decide if anyone gets anything at all."

James liked hearing her vent. Keeping all that bottled up had to be feeding her panic attacks. Listening to her talk about it meant she had a release, and she trusted him enough to share her real life with him.

"I really liked Charlotte" she continued. "There were plenty of things to do there and people were higher quality than here."

"So you lived in Charlotte? I grew up there. There and Rock Hill. I was a lifeguard at Carowinds."

"I could see you doing that."

"We grew up next to a lake, and all we

ever did was swim all summer long. So when I got a summer job, life guard just came natural." Casey turned the hot water on with her foot.

"Why don't you get out, honey. I'll go fix the couch up for us to watch a movie."

"I just want to go to bed."

"That's ok too." James smiled at her. "We've never had sex at your house."

"I don't want to have sex. I just want to lay on my heating pad. My back is killing me."

"Ok, hun. Would you like me to stay or go home?"

"I want you to stay, but you can go if you want to."

James leaned over the tub and kissed her on the forehead. "I don't ever want to leave you. I have never found someone that I could talk to like we talk. You don't have any idea how much I enjoy your company. I wish we didn't live so far apart. Leave the water in the tub, and I'll bathe before coming to bed."

"Yuck! You can take a shower. This water is dirty."

"That's fine too." When James came out of the shower and had dried off, he walked into the bedroom. Casey was under flannel bed sheets. She had a heating pad under her and was wearing a sleep mask." James wondered should he just let her sleep, but she seemed like she really wanted him there. He hoped his snoring wouldn't wake her. It didn't.

Meeting his Mother & Brother

"Love, you know, seeks to make happy rather than to be happy." – Ralph Connor

Casey didn't seem excited or unexcited. She had started just fitting in and being part of the family. "She is a wonderful addition," thought James and his mother would later say the same thing about her.

Casey had spent the night before with him, and James had the whole crew. Like she promised, she went with them to Pembroke College and met his mother, step-father and brother. James' nephew was part of his schools chorus and they performed at the half time of a basketball game.

James' brother seemed scared of Casey, but his step-father was very approving. Casey warmed up quickly to them all, and she was very polite and charming. James wondered if there was a limit to how many people she could be around before she had a panic attack. Apparently the answer was more than three.

James' mother was very gentle and polite. Casey was nothing but smiles. It was a long trip especially carrying all the kids with them. But when they returned home, they really felt like a family come home. Casey helped getting everyone to bed. She showed the first signs of really being a part of a wonderful family.

Casey tucked the girls in and kissed them good night.

Things Become More Daily

"Winter is the time for comfort, for good food and warmth, for the touch of a friendly hand and for a talk beside the fire: it is the time for home." – Edith Sitwell

James sat at his own dining room table Thursday with his girls. They talked about school and the upcoming Church play. He was happy they loved him so much. He knew he was a great Dad. That feeling was reinforced by all the new parents that asked him for parenting advice. If he had done anything wrong, it was to spoil them too much, if that's possible. After dinner he asked Jamie to do the dishes while he took the little ones back to their mother's.

"Dad," began Jamie, "after I do this can I go over to Lindsey's?"

"Sure. You gonna be there a while or just a little bit?"

"For a while. I'll be back by bedtime."

"Well, if you are leaving me for the evening, would you mind if I went to see Casey? I can come home tonight if you want me too."

"No, that's ok."

"Well, you are going to your mother's after school and spend the weekend? Do you want me to be here for anything? Otherwise I will just pack and stay with Casey till Sunday and meet you here when you come home?"

"That's cool with me." Jamie smiled. "I'm glad you have a girl friend."

"Are you sure? We don't get to talk like we used to, but that's only because I don't have to drive you places. You drive yourself now. I miss all our talks."

"We can talk Sunday. Love you daddy."

"Love you too, baby. You got enough gas?" James handed her twenty dollars. "If you need any more, ask your mom for some money. You don't have to tell her I just gave you some." Jamie hugged her Dad tight and smiled.

James texted as he walked out to his van. He asked Casey if he could spend the rest of the week with her. He already had a bag packed and in the van. She didn't always return a text right away. By the time he had dropped his kids off, she had replied telling him it was okay.

He got to her house about 10 minutes before she got there. He had brought some movies and something to read while she was at work tomorrow. She came home and didn't look happy. Casey said that she had had a very bad and long day. She complained that her feet hurt, her calves hurt, and her back hurt. She went to the bathroom and came out more angry than when she went in.

"What's wrong, honey?"

"I just hurt. I am tired of hurting." Her face twisted up, and she started to cry. James wrapped his arms around her and hugged her gently. He wanted to tell her to quit working as a stripper. That it was sucking the life out of her, but he wasn't sure yet. He knew he loved her. No one had ever made him feel so alive, so wanted. James wanted to do more for her, but he couldn't. He was just getting his own life put back together. How he wished she had come into his life two years ago. With her by his side, things would have been very different.

James had noticed that Casey took a lot of pain medications. At first he had thought maybe one of the waitresses had been right claiming that Casey would zombie out because of pain meds. But he had interacted with her for nearly two months, and it seemed that something else fueled her anxiety. Now that she had him, she didn't seem anxious very often at all. Her only episodes were when she came home from work and would complain that she was better than this. She was right. College educated, personable, communicative and creative. James wondered why she had not had more success already, but he was grateful for whatever life had delivered her to him.

James had fixed them dinner and while they ate, the phone rang. She looked at it and then switched it off. Her mood soured. "Who was that?"

"The people I borrowed money for my car from. They keep harassing me, calling over and over and won't stop."

"Are you behind on your payments?"

"I was broke and out of work for six months, I got behind, but I made my last payment."

James was a fixer. He wasn't going to pay his new girlfriends bills for her but he would help her if he could. "I had this problem with Dell Computer Company. I know how to make them stop calling you if you want me to show you. But if you trust me, I will look at your bill and see if we can fix it."

Casey brought him all her mail and notices. Then she went into the bedroom and ran herself a bath. James looked over the bills and it only took three minutes to see that she was 4 ½ months behind. No wonder they called her all the time.

James walked into the bathroom and sat in his usual spot on the floor next to the tub. "Honey, it's your fault that they call so often, but that doesn't mean they are allowed to harass you. All you have to do is tell them to stop by sending a certified mail. Just ignoring them won't accomplish anything.

Casey made a face and James knew it was because he told her it was her fault. "Honey, I think we can get you in good favor if you just make an adjustment to your payments instead of trying to pay it all at once." James remembered helping her count her money from being a stripper. Apparently, stripping pays very well. "You know, you have enough money to just pay it off and then you will save nearly eighteen hundred dollars in interest."

"No!" Casey snapped. "That would be all of my money and I wouldn't have any left. They shouldn't be allowed to take my money anyway. They screwed me over with a twenty four percent loan because I owe student loans and have bad credit. They have been robbing me for four years now."

James pursed his lips and rolled his mouth to the side. "I don't disagree with you at all, but you signed the contract. You agreed to the deal and so you have to pay them."

"No I don't. They are crooks."

James snickered, and she cut her eyes at him, "Do you want me to talk to them and see if I can straighten it out for you?"

Casey stared at him a long time and didn't speak. A few minutes went by and James went back into the living room and stacked everything neatly into a pile. Casey walked up to him naked and then wrapped herself in a house coat. "You can call them but I want to listen."

"Of course, I will have to get you to talk to them at some point." The two of them called, and James negotiated until Casey nodded her head and then handed the phone over to her. She had one less stressor in her life. James thought that was a good and great step of helping her anxieties. She snuggled with him tightly that night, and they made love.

Friday, Casey got up and went to work. He promised to have dinner ready for her when she got home. They had stayed up to the wee hours of the morning, and although it was 10:30 he wanted to sleep some more. Casey left for work and James snored for two more hours.

When James woke up, he lay in her bed and stared at the ceiling. She had found some intimate time with him last night despite her aches and pains. He loved the way she had come to make love to him. She liked to play and tease like a ritual dance. It was an exchange of desires and not just some dead activity like his marriage had been for twenty years.

He grabbed her pillow and laid it over his face. He could smell her perfume on it and only made him miss her more. He rolled over and looked at the clock on the wall. It didn't work. It was always 4:15. He thought maybe he would put some batteries in it. He looked at her night stand beside the bed. On the bottom shelf was a colorful book that looked like patches and had a large sun on it. He picked it up and opened it. She had written poems in the first few pages. He read one and then another. They reminded him of his own poetry from high school. He flipped to the center and saw that it had a diary entry. He thought to read it, but then decided if she wanted him to know she would tell him. So he laid the book on the top of the nightstand and rolled back over and hugged her pillow. James couldn't wait for her to come home.

She came home and seemed to be in good spirits. He had dinner made and they shared another long conversation about nothing and everything. She made him laugh, and he made her snort. Together they were like old friends reunited, the energy was exciting.

After dinner she went and took a shower. After her shower she came into the living room with a towel around her. "Do you miss me when I'm gone?"

"I definitely do" James said emphatically.

She smiled at him and let the towel drop to the floor. "Don't you wish you could see this all day?"

James laughed, "I do. But I like the fact that we get along so well even without the sex. But I do love the way you flirt."

"Get your phone and take a picture of me." Casey stretched out across the carpet. She rolled and stretched and teased him sensually.

James had never taken pictures of his wife or any other girlfriend, not like this. She loved the attention and wanted him to capture her from every angle. "You like to paint! I always wanted a painting of my body stretched out over a wide narrow canvas. Maybe you will paint that for me?"

"I would love too. But I am afraid it would never catch your true beauty. I would be afraid I might disappoint you. You are a better artist than me. Take this picture and you sketch your form out. You like to model, don't you."

"I used to model in college." She hopped up naked and her body was tight but her boobs bounced. It was exhilarating. She went over to a box that had sat next to the wall for two months. Casey pulled out sheets of negatives of slides. In them you could see her posing one way or another. She looked much younger, but she was far more beautiful now. She sat in his lap and tried to keep his interest on the slides and her stories, but she was naked and in his lap and she was all he had thought of all day. He had not imagined this is what the night would yield, but he was excited and pleased. Casey noticed he wasn't listening anymore; he was too distracted by her lack of clothes.

"You want me don't you?"

"Of course I do. And you are just teasing me."

"I am not just teasing you. She stood up and took his hand and led him to the bedroom." James went into the bathroom and brushed his teeth. He was excited and his heart was beating a million miles a minute. They had been making love several times a week, and it just kept getting better. It felt as if she really loved him and wanted to make him happy every way that she could. And he knew he wanted to make her happy and he loved that he never had to guess. She stopped him if she didn't like something and she prompted him when she wanted something. They were a team and they each wanted to make the other happy. James rinsed his mouth and smiled in the mirror, turned and walked into the bedroom.

Casey was sitting on the corner of the bed dressed in pjs. She had a scowl on her face, and she looked at him angrily.

"What's wrong honey?"

"You snooped all through my house while I was at work and went through everything I owned." She was angry, almost mad over it.

"I think you might be mistaken. I did look at your closet and laughed at the number of shoes you owned, but all I was doing was getting your clothes size to get you a Christmas present that would fit properly. How could you even tell?"

Casey looked at him even more angrily then pointed at the book on top of the night stand. "You went through my things and read about me! These are my private thoughts!"

He realized now that he had taken the book from the bottom of the nightstand and then laid it on the top.

"Honey, I wasn't snooping. I just picked it up cause it was within arm's reach, and when I saw you had written a dairy like page I set it down."

"You read my diary?" Casey was inconsolable. She fussed at him for an hour and he finally apologized for the tenth time or more and went into the living room and lay on the couch to go to sleep. About thirty minutes passed when she came out to the couch and she poked him hard.

"What?!" he snapped at her.

"I want you to come to bed."

"So you can yell at me some more."

"No." and then she turned and walked back to the bedroom. James lay there about three minutes and then got up and walked into the bedroom. She was curled up in the bed, mask on, heating pad searing and decked out in thick pajamas. He was disappointed she was angry with him. Not a good way to start a weekend. He undressed and got in bed. He hated her bed. It was too hard, too low, and her covers were not to his liking. She rolled over and spooned him and squeezed him tightly. He loved her bed. He smiled, squeezed her arm, and they fell asleep.

The Holidays 2010

"The Christmas spirit – love – changes hearts and lives." – Pat Boone

It went from happy to sad like a rollercoaster. One of Casey's family friends had died from cancer. She had just texted him a few days before and laughed and shared stories about him with James explaining that he was her mother's friend and that he was like an extra grandfather to her. She loved talking to him and he being in her life. Now he was gone. She didn't want to go to the funeral. She thought he was going to be cremated anyway. For someone who seemed so important to her one minute, he was not mentioned again. Maybe it was the distraction of her new life and the happiness she was experiencing. James hoped so.

The two of them went Christmas shopping, and Casey said she was taking a few days off from work and wanted to spend them with him. He told her that he had the kids after Christmas, but she was still welcome to join them as a family.

Casey and James were a match. James loved to spoil people, and Casey loved to be spoiled. The attention James gave Casey was loving and genuine, and Casey returned his love with laughter and smiles. James wondered why he had had to wait so long to find someone that could just fill his heart up with joy, just by being in the same room.

Casey came on the weekends, and James visited her during the week. It was always the same but in a very good way. She arrived looking tired, grumpy and worn down, but in just a few minutes she would light up and fill the room radiantly.

One dinner just before Christmas, Jamie sat with Casey and James. The banter was of the usual sort, and James felt happy to see his new family coming together. When the meal was over, Jamie asked "Dad, if I save up my own money, can I go to California and stay with Jennifer for a month?"

James did not hesitate, "I doubt that. Who is Jennifer? And what are we talking about?"

Jamie showed considerable enthusiasm, "She is my girlfriend; we talk online all the time. She likes all the same things I do, and I really like her. We want to visit and go to an anime convention."

"Honey, I don't think so. You are asking me to let you go three thousand miles away to live with a family I have never met to be with a girl than you are romantically interested in. I wouldn't even let your sister stay out past eleven with her boyfriend across town. I just don't see how this is safe or responsible. Maybe we can plan something, and we all go to the Anime Convention together."

Jamie was angry. That was not what she wanted, and she twisted her face up, "Forget it. I don't know why you can't trust me."

"Wait honey, it isn't that I don't trust you. It's because I want you to be safe. It's because I love you and don't want bad things to happen to you." James tried to reach out to touch her, but she pulled away. Jamie did not speak of it again.

Christmas morning came, and they had plans to eat breakfast at James' best friend's house. Usually he had all the kids in tow, but this morning they were at their mom's and it was him and his new family, Casey. James could not wait for them to meet her.

She was slow to get ready, and James tried to lighten her mood. She seemed purposefully stalling to not have to go, as if he would go without her and save her the effort. But James waited patiently and then she was ready.

Dressed in white, she never had to try to be beautiful. Casey just was. She came in with a sullen sad expression but James' friends would have nothing of the sort. They grabbed her and hugged her and welcomed her in to the fold. If James liked her they would too. But things made a quick turn south when it was discovered that there was no coffee. James offered to go get some, but his host insisted that he come along as well. It was not a big deal, but it was inconvenient. Momma (the matriarch of this adoptive family was 36 when James met her at 17, she's been his mama ever since) was a little taken aback, but she didn't say anything. They returned soon with coffee enough for all.

Christmas breakfast was an elaborate spread, and as the women of the house got things in order for the meal, James and Casey sat on the couch and talked with the male members of the family. Casey discussed sports with them, and they all made fun of James lack of sport knowledge. She warmed up to them quickly and giggled and smiled as the stories were tossed around. James friends mostly were trying to embarrass him knowing that wasn't possible. Soon momma called everyone to breakfast.

Everyone was there. They had three grown kids and their kids had kids. James was like the adopted son and only added to the extended family. As they gathered around the table, Casey lifted up a coffee cup and examined the bottom. A disapproving look came across her face. James asked Casey if she wanted something and she nodded and went into the kitchen. He followed her, and she found it odd that he knew his way around their house like it was his own.

They joined everyone for Christmas Brunch, and the stories flowed just like every Christmas before.

Around noon they left to go home and wait for James' kids. When they arrived, they opened presents, and laughed and then they ran out and played in the snow. When James came back in the house, Casey had made everyone hot chocolate.

That night they played together with all the Christmas toys, and they laughed. The house once again was filled with love from every angle. Casey was just what the family needed, and in some ways it looked like she needed them too.

That night she didn't dress in her usual heavy pj's. She was much softer and sexy. She smiled at James and whispered, "You have one more gift to unwrap." James couldn't wait, when she loved him, she loved him very well and it was all the moments in between the act that made his heart soar. She gazed in his eyes, scratched gently across his skin, teased him and tickled him and then rewarded his patience and gentle touch. Casey's love was the very best Christmas gift ever.

At breakfast she was wearing one of his shirts. It didn't fit her but she looked so very sexy in his clothes. The idea that she wanted to be wrapped up with him all day long was so sexy James could hardly contain his enthusiasm. Casey made the whole family breakfast and James tried to stay out of her way and get in her way for a kiss all at the same time. Her bright smile filled the house with love that had been missing for years and years. James hoped that this feeling was going to last and he told himself not to be afraid to enjoy every minute. Every time he could, he found a way to kiss her again and again.

The kids loved her and so did James. As they all sat around the table sipping chocolate and chatting, James couldn't help but notice Casey. She seemed sad at one of the most joyous moments of his life. He couldn't help but wonder how her life was growing up. Did her family have big fancy shindigs? Was she missing those memories now? Her mood did not improve, and she seemed to almost sulk. James divided his attention between her and the kids, his daughters getting the lion's share. When the opportunity for him to take a breather came and daddy could stop being a jungle gym, James plopped down on the couch. Casey came over and sat in his lap. James looked her soft face. It was not as bright or glowing but she was still beautiful, but she just looked worried.

"What would you like for dinner? I was thinking we could heat up the left-over turkey and make sandwiches."

Casey pursed her lips, "I think I will go home." James had hoped she felt home her with him and his family, and his heart sank.

"Something wrong?"

"No. You just seem very busy, and the kids want your attention."

"Well, that's what kids do. I love to spoil them, and they love that you are here." Casey looked around the living room at the front door. James wondered what had gone wrong today. It seemed like a wonderful day that just slipped slowly into mediocrity. Casey was polite, but she was also determined, and soon she walked out and drove home.

Looking out into the snow as she drove

away, suddenly he felt cold in her absence. James played with his kids but his heart was missing Casey. Over the week he called her and texted her and reminded her she was going to be his date for New Year's Party at the same home they had had Thanksgiving dinner. She promised she would be there.

December 31st they made desserts and James called Casey to make sure everything was still good. She said she would be there. James knew it was a silly tradition but he really wanted to kiss her under the mistletoe at midnight. He really wanted to kiss her every night. His life had gone from average to amazing, and it was all because of Casey. For his New Year's resolution he decided that he was going to find some new way to regain his old income back. He did not like being on a strict budget, and he wasn't used to it.

James had always loved exploring the world, but his ex-wife Carol had been an anchor he had to drag along. Casey was curious and wide eyed. She wanted to explore and experience too. He snorted as he thought, why couldn't she have come along first and these be their wonderful kids. But then he paused and realized that they would be completely different if that were the case and he was very proud of his children. He wouldn't want anyone of them to change. Nothing was better than being a proud parent. Then he felt sad.

James wondered if Casey wanted kids. She was twelve years younger than him and still had time. He already had four and was forty-three; any new kids would make him very old as a father. Plus, his new financial situation would make it difficult in all aspects. But still he wondered. If she wanted kids, he didn't want to deprive her of that experience. He was going to have to sit down and talk with her. James was happy, but if she had some lifelong dream that he wasn't aware of, then he needed to know so that he could adjust. James was certain he didn't want more kids. His heart grew heavy thinking that might divide them. His heavy heart would grow as the night progressed.

Casey didn't show up at seven as they had planned. He called and she said she was behind schedule. James wondered if the week six days apart had left her feeling abandoned. He called her again at nine, but there was no answer. She called him back at ten saying she couldn't remember where it was. James was imagining that she was zoning out and going into panic attacks. He remained as calm as he could and gently coaxed her into leaving her house. She did not make it to the party; he missed his opportunity to kiss her under the mistletoe. But she was waiting for him when they got home. She was lying on the couch and he went straight to her and lifted her up and kissed her. James did not admonish her for not coming to the party.

"I missed you this week. I missed you tonight." He squeezed her hands tightly. Her eyes were filled with sadness and worry.

James tilted his head and smiled, "I love you Casey. This is going to be a great year for us." A small smile came across her face. "Come help me get them in bed." Casey climbed the stairs and helped put the little ones under covers giving everyone kisses.

January 2011

Casey completely missed the New Year's Party, although she was at James' house when he arrived home. She commented that she just didn't want to be around anyone, that they made her uncomfortable but that she wanted to be with him and had come to sleep. James although disappointed, understood the difficulties she had expressed so often but he also recognized the progress she had shown. He was glad that she had come to trust him to be in her life. He knew that she was a long way from being healthy but he wasn't looking for anything more than a friend to share part of his life with and now he had a girlfriend that he cherished. Maybe he hoped she might one day be better. Maybe, just maybe this younger woman would see the value and worth in him and stick around. He was happy she was his girlfriend. She had very quickly become his best friend and favorite person.

For his birthday, James invited all his friends to dinner at a restaurant an hour away from his town. But only ten minutes for Casey. The weatherman began predicting gloom and doom and an impending snow storm and so one by one his friends texted to say they wouldn't be coming, until finally, James finished his meal alone. The manager of the restaurant took pity on him and gave him his meal for free. James laughed and thanked him, then commented on how well the server had tried to make him feel better. James left a generous tip.

When James finished, he drove over to Casey's house. She opened the door and let him in even though he had a key of his own.

James cupped her face and lifted her chin. Her eyes looked sad; she knew she had disappointed him. It was his birthday. James was learning that Casey did not function well in social gatherings. She could sit around strangers and even interact one on one. When it came time to be part of a group, she was paralyzed with fear. "It's ok. We are together now." A hint of smile came across her face and they snuggled up on the couch under a blanket and felt warm and safe together.

Casey fell asleep first. She always did. James was happy she felt so safe with him. He didn't want to hurt her or use her. He loved loving her and seeing the wonder and appreciation that she returned to him. Watching her with other people, James could see that she was very defensive and paranoid. She would be short with others and often was put-offish. But with him, she was vulnerable and open. He didn't want to do anything to violate her trust, to compromise her security. She pretended to be strong, but she was very fragile.

What had he wanted for his birthday? Friends, presents, party? Yes, but he had those things each time for years and not just on his birthday. What James really wanted was a partner in life that appreciated him and wanted to be next to him. He looked down at Casey and kissed the top of her head. She was everything he always wanted. He wondered how it was going to keep it all together, his life. James needed to find a way to get back to his previous income, not just for Casey or his kids, but for himself. He realized that the hopelessness he had been trying not to feel as a result of his disease had been winning. Casey had saved him from that. Her presence was the motivation he needed to propel himself back into being successful. He had done it once. He could do it again.

Two mornings later, James looked out his bedroom window. He sat in front of his computer and tried to make a plan to get back into the world. James had been sick for years but he was beginning to feel better. He was limited, but he was not crippled. James looked at Casey's picture on his phone, her smile so wide and bright. He was going to make his life better. He was going to make their life better. He wasn't sure what she saw in him. He was at his lifetime worst. He was way overweight, diseased and on disability. James was on a very restrictive budget that was getting tighter as he spent money every day on gas to drive back and forth to see her. He was glad Casey loved him. He just didn't know why she did. Then he thought, does she love me? Had she ever said that she loved him. Casey showed him physical attention and intimate moments, and James realized that she had expressed love by her daily actions but he wasn't sure she had ever said it. He wondered was she afraid.

James opened his computer and decided to write his feelings down.

As I look warmly upon you today
I wonder what words could convey
Truth about what tomorrow could bring
If only you would allow your heart to sing

For here there are no riches to wear
No gold nor diamond tiara for your hair

Absent are the servants many
Bills and debt are a gracious plenty

But here inside these simple walls
True love whispers, true love calls
A simple gesture of flowers I bring
If only you would allow your heart to sing

Pearls and lockets, or emerald bracelet
Wealth eludes me, I cannot fake it
Dream if you must of jewelry galore
But life's no game there is no score

Come with me and what you will find
Is an endless love in this heart of mine
Fountain of adoration, a wondrous spring
If only you would allow your heart to sing

Promises in the dark are made by men
Who long to commit original sin
Who only want to feel your affection
Without concern for your heart's reflection

But here in the absence of your touch
Grows a love still that has grown so much
Passion for her actions as she does her thing
If only you would allow your heart to sing

Paradise plenty is not where I live
I have no treasures for which to give
Material things that bring brief pleasure
I possess too little to bother to measure

Find yourself some serenity
Know that love is a firm security
That unlocks the soul and sets it free
Rest gently in my chair with me

Not for a minute, an hour or a day
Forever is how long I wish you to stay
You'd be my Queen and I'd be your King
If only you would allow your heart to sing

James finished the poem and realized that he did love Casey and that he wanted her not just today but every day. That she loved him in his worst, and he loved her in her worst. Together they could heal and build a life that would make other people jealous. James was suddenly terrified.

Casey was still stripping at the club and although she hated it, she was making a lot of money. It gave her security and stability. She still had trouble paying her bills but not because Casey lacked money but because she felt wronged by the collectors. It was a very odd thing to James, but she had asked him for his opinions and help. He had used her money to get her back into a proper cycle.

This was important. Casey had not tried to get James to buy her anything ever. He had never been her customer at the club. She invited him into her life because she saw some value in him and now two and half months later, James did not want to imagine a life without her. But how would he make it all work. He would find a way. He always did.

During the day, James went to the State's rehabilitation office and asked them yet again for help getting a job or an education for a new job. They dragged their feet so often but he kept pushing and finally they were making some baby steps. He wanted this now more than ever. He wanted to get his life productive and profitable. James wanted Casey to be part of it and continue to make it wonderful. They both deserved a better life. James knew in that moment he wanted her to be his wife.

That night when she came home, James asked her if she would like to go shopping. She shrugged her shoulders and said ok. She then disappeared in the bedroom and changed clothes quickly. When she walked into the kitchen to go, James was standing beside the table.

"I have never done this before." James said nervously. Casey looked at him odd. "I want to go shopping with you." James wondered should he get down on a knee or stand and look her in the eye. James had nothing to give her but not because he hadn't thought about it, but because he wanted her to have exactly what she wanted. "Casey, I love you and I want you to marry me." He squeezed her hands, the look on her face was not joy but concern, "I didn't buy you a ring because I want you to help me pick it out. That is why I want to go shopping."

Casey seemed utterly confused. "You want me to marry you?" she stammered.

"Yes, very much. I do. I want to spend the rest of life making you happy, the way you make me happy. Would you marry a man like me?"

Casey looked frightened and then a soft smile swept across her face, "Yes." She nodded as well.

James smiled, "Well then, let's go shopping and see if we can find you a ring that you want to wear." The two of them went to the malls and looked in one jewelry store and then another. Casey picked up books and advertisements. She didn't seem to see anything she really wanted. "I want it to be unique, not just a diamond, but something personal and special to me."

James nodded in agreement, "I want you to pick it out because I want you to love it. I love you Casey. You have already made me the happiest man in the world. Now let me make you the happiest woman."

James returned to her house the next night. All the catalogues and brochures they had gotten were still lying on the kitchen table in the same spot he had left them. Casey couldn't have been too excited if she hadn't even looked at them again. He tried not read too much into it. It was late when they got home and she had left right after they woke up. Still, James couldn't resist the temptation to look at them so he wondered why she could.

Casey came home from work in a very good mood. James had made dinner, and she sat down and started talking about this customer that had been coming in regularly to see her. "Keith is from Virginia. He drives all the way here to see me once a week. He spends a lot of money on me every time he comes in." James didn't care. He had more than a few stripper friends, and they weren't all prostitutes. Casey certainly wasn't.

"Well, I 'm glad you had a good day for a change. I hate when you come home all burned out and angry."

"Keith asked me to spend Super Bowl weekend with him. He is going to pay me eight hundred dollars." Suddenly, James cared.

"That's not a good idea, Casey."

"Why not? He is a good guy. He always treats me right and pays me a lot."

James shook his head, "Because it's not safe. Because if what you call yourself is an entertainer because you dance provocatively, well that's one thing, but if you go for the weekend; well, that's something else. That is more escorting and if he is going to pay you eight hundred dollars, his expectations will be more than you just watching football with him, and that would be prostitution. You already hate your job, do you really want to go further down that dark path?"

"He has more money than he has sense and he claims to have it in his house. If I go, I could find out where he keeps it, and we could rob him." James paused. Who was this person sitting across from him?

"Have you been drinking?" asked James. "Did you really just suggest that you take an escort job to scout a man's house so we could rob him?" James was visibly upset. He looked at her, and she looked away pouty.

"I just want to be able to get out of debt."

"Well, that is not the way you do it." James felt like a hypocrite. He often fantasized about he could rob different people to better his life, but he had never actually asked someone to help him. There seemed to be a line between reality and fantasy that he had never crossed, but she just did. She was visibly angry that he told her she couldn't spend the weekend with Keith. James decided to divert the conversation and slide a book across the table toward her. "Did you look at any of these?"

She opened the book and flipped to a specific page. "I like this one a little but I am not sure." So she had looked through the book enough to have picked a favorite. He walked over beside her and looked at what she was looking at. "If I go this weekend, we would have enough money for a ring."

"We already have enough money for a reasonable ring. And if you start escorting, you won't need a ring you will need a new boyfriend." She dropped the book on the table and disappeared into the bedroom. James walked around the table and started cleaning up dinner plates. This was not the way he had planned to spend his evening.

Casey came out of the bedroom naked and told him to make some coffee. Then she disappeared into her bathroom. James made her coffee and then brought it to her. She scooted up and for the first time offered him a place in her bath. James peeled away his clothes and sank down into the water with her. She leaned back against him. "I just want you to be safe. If you go spend a weekend with some customer for that amount of money, and then you don't put out, he might get angry and hurt you. At least at the club there are bouncers to protect you. Honestly I don't really like you working at the club. Not because I am judgmental but because you seem to hate it so much. You find it degrading."

"I hate it." Casey sipped her coffee.

"You don't have to work there you know." James rubbed her shoulders. "We don't have a fortune but between us we can make it easily till August, maybe September. But sometime before then, you would need to find some small job that would bring in just a little."

Casey didn't say anything. "I love you Casey. I want you to be safe and happy." She pushed herself hard against him and they talked until the water was cold. Then they dried off and went to bed with the sleep mask and the heating pad.

When morning came, she asked him was he going to stay. "I need to go home but I can be back before you get home from work."

"Ok, I need to get ready." James kissed her good bye and then left and drove home. It was just a regular day, but there were still things to get accomplished. His favorite was bringing the Anime Club a big spread to eat for their meetings. He didn't have to do it. He did it because the club was important to Jamie, and James loved to spoil her.

Today they were watching another anime movie that to him looked pretty much like all the rest of them. The girls shushed him three times, and he got up and walked over to Jamie. "What are your plans for the evening?"

"I was going to go to Abby's house. Is that ok?"

"Sure. Do you mind if I go back to Casey's?"

"Nope. I will see you tomorrow?"

"Yes, and I was going to ask Casey to stay with us this weekend if you don't mind?"

"That's fine."

"She loves anime too, you know. She was telling me about Ouran High School or something like that. Of course I love the fact that she has a Marvin the Martian Doll and a Brain Doll from Pinky and the Brain."

"She seems cool, daddy. I like her."

"I do too." James hesitated. He wanted to tell Jamie that he asked Casey to marry him but now that she was talking about robbing Keith, he was a little scared himself.

He arrived at her apartment and made dinner. She didn't arrive at her normal time. He waited until the food was cold and then he cleaned up. Sitting down at the table he looked at the clock. She was two hours late. He called the club and asked if she were there, but they said no. James walked around her apartment and looked out the window into the parking lot. Perhaps she was angry about him telling her she couldn't go away for the weekend. He waited by the window about a half hour. His confusion turned to anger. She had invited him over. It wasn't like he just showed up unannounced. Then his anger turned to worry.

James walked out to his van and drove to her bank. Often Casey would stop by there and deposit money she earned from the day. He looked for her car and then got out and walked around looking for any sign of struggle. Nothing. James got back in the van and drove back to her apartment. She still had not arrived home. He waited a half hour more. Then he called the club again, and again they said she wasn't there.

James panicked; he called 911 and asked if Casey's car had come up on any accidents. They told him no and asked if he wanted to file a missing person's report. He said he didn't, but when they asked how long she had been missing he said almost five hours now. They recommended he make the report so they could start the clock in case it was needed. He didn't want to. She didn't want anyone to know what she did for a living. She definitely didn't want a police report stating what she did. But then again, what she did for a living placed her at considerable risk.

When they called back a half hour later, he relented and they made an incident report. An officer went by the Men's Club and asked if anyone had seen her leave, or if maybe she left with someone. While that was going on, she came home. It was almost two in the morning. James was heart-broken. She had been out drinking.

James picked up the phone and called the police, "She's home." He listened, "Ok." Casey looked at him and gave a quirky smile.

"Who was that?"

"It was the police. I had them looking for you because I thought you had been in an accident. I have called all the hospitals, drove by your bank machine, the club, and waited here."

She looked confused, "Why would you do any of that? Why did you call the police?" She looked like she wanted to be angry but was too tipsy to get angry.

"The question is why did you ask me to be here when you got home and then you not come home?" James was definitely not happy.

"I went out with a customer that wanted to give me a job. Here is his card."

"If he wanted to give you a job, he would have told you to come by his office, not meet him at a bar." James looked at the card and then sat it on the table. "Honey, that wasn't safe. You can't run off with customers and disappear. Yes, I know strippers do it all the time, but they always take another girl with them as a back-up."

"I am not a stripper. I am an exotic dancer."

"You take your clothes off for money and crawl on top of men pressing your body against theirs to make them want you to stay longer and buy more attention. I am sorry honey, but you are a stripper. But you don't have to be. You claim you hate it."

"I do hate it." She snapped. "I have a college degree, damn it. But I couldn't find a job using it." She would have said more but a knock came at the door. James got up and walked to answer it.

He told the officer that she had come home, and the officer insisted he talk to her since a report was made. James called her to the door, but she wouldn't come. He asked the officer to step into the entry hall. "Honey, he's not going to leave till he sees identification." Casey's eyes pierced James like daggers. James walked into the living room and sat down in her chair.

After talking with the officer, she showed him out and then went into the bedroom. James sulked in the chair trying to decide if he should go home. He couldn't understand why she was suddenly a different person. He had just about decided it wasn't worth the effort when Casey called out from the bedroom, "Are you coming to bed?"

James didn't answer right away. He huffed and puffed and his brain raced at all the things he should do. "No," he said finally, "I think I will go home."

Casey came out of the bedroom quickly and climbed into the chair on top of him. She snuggled up against him like a cat, using her whole body to tempt him. James was angry and hurt. But Casey was persistent. James made a move to leave and she plopped down on him to put him back in the chair. Her eyes met his and she stared deep into them. She was more alluring now than ever before. Casey looked genuinely concerned that she had messed up. He waited for her to say she was sorry, but it didn't seem to be coming. He moved to get up again, "Where are you going"

"Home. It's apparent you don't care about me or our relationship or why would you have done this? You didn't answer your phone. You didn't respond to a text. You treated me with complete disrespect and made me worry for nothing, so you could go out drinking with some customer who lured you away with the promise of a job but took you to a bar. And you think that's intelligent and safe. And after all this, you haven't even bothered to say that you are sorry."

Casey looked at him sorrowful. She knew she had really let him down and she looked genuinely concerned. He went to get up again, she pushed him down "I'm sorry."

"I am too. I thought you loved me."

"I do."

"You do what?" James looked at her his nostrils still flaring.

"I do love you. She put her hand on his chest. I am really sorry. Please don't go." She didn't seem tipsy any more. She seemed stone sober. James couldn't decide what he wanted. He glanced over at the brochures of wedding rings and wondered if she was acting out because she didn't want to get married. He looked at the floor and shook his head, and then he looked at her.

"Are you sure? Sure you love me?"

"Yes." She looked at each of his eyes.

"Then tell me."

"I am sure that I love you."

"No, tell me that you won't treat me like this again. I would never treat you this way."

She never stopped looking into his eyes. This was the first time she had ever seemed so confident. James wondered if it was liquid courage. "I promise I won't do this again. Please don't leave me. I do love you."

James picked her up and started carrying her to the bedroom. The Meniere's disease made it very difficult, and he slammed her ankle into the door frame. She yelped and started cussing at him for being a cripple but in a playful way. He dumped her on the bed and turned out the lights.

James didn't make it Thursday night, but Casey came to his house on Friday and spent the weekend. She was so cheerful when she was separated from her home. At his house she laughed and played and interacted; at hers, she was brooding and still had an occasional panic attack.

Casey lay across the bed and told him about how her aunt had thrown her out and called her an alcoholic. Now she had come home drunk and been irresponsible just two days before, but James had a stocked bar in his house and neither one of them ever made a drink from it. In fact the only person that ever seemed to use it was his brother. James did not think Casey to have a drinking problem. It had been over three months and she had only one incident of irresponsibility. He still wondered did all those behaviors come about because he asked her to marry him. It was very early, maybe he had rushed her, and she was pushing back.

Casey wasn't completely drug free. She did seem to take a lot of pain killers, but they had been prescription so someone thought she needed them. After they were used up, James had given her a few of his and then started giving her over the counter pain killers. She complained that they were useless and what she really needed was a chiropractor. James looked in the phonebook, and they picked one out. Turns out, that was exactly what she needed. Two visits later she would stop complaining and stop taking pain medications. However, just before that everything would change.

A New Beginning

"In every life a little rain must fall..."

Casey came home Monday night, and she was distraught. The weekend had been a wonderful family experience, and James had renewed faith in having asked her to marry him. He told his daughter Jamie and she approved. Casey had spent the weekend being part of her new family. She fit right in. Monday night she came home from the club and sat down at the table.

James had made quail for dinner, something different and a little bit exotic. Casey looked at the meal and commented that the chicken looked particularly puny. James laughed and indicated that they were living a bit posh and described his shopping experience for that afternoon. But Casey seemed disinterested, and she moved the plate towards the center of the table. She had been so happy all weekend, and now eight hours at the club, and she looked like she was about to fall all to pieces.

"What is it honey? What's wrong?"

"My life sucks. Everything about my life is wrong and horrible."

"Wait just a minute! I would beg to differ. I am in your life. Are you calling me horrible and our relationship wrong?"

"No." her face drew up like a raisin and she fought back tears. "You are the only thing right in my life. But I am not supposed to work there. I am better than this. They hate me and I hate them. Why did I go to college to end up like this? I don't even want to live. I just want to die and it all be over." Casey plopped forward and her head made a loud thump against the table. James didn't know what to say. His heart felt like it was being wrapped tightly by some restraining wire. Casey began lifting her face up and then slamming it against the table. James froze and then she slammed her head down again. He hopped up and ran around the table.

Grabbing Casey's shoulders James lifted her higher. "Honey! Honey! Stop. Just stop." He began to console her and whisper. She turned her face into his chest, and he held her tightly as she wept. "Casey, you can't keep living like this. You are two different people. When you were at my house, you were happy and loving and bright and cheerful, and here in your own home in this world, you are so dark and angry and sad." It seemed so obvious to James but he didn't know how he could make it all work. James wanted to try. He needed to do something to save the woman he loved and the love that had been born between them. James knelt down on his knee and got under her face so she could see him. Her makeup was being washed away by a constant flow of tears. "Casey? Honey? Do you love me?"

Him questioning her did not make Casey feel better. Of course she loved him. She had told him so. Casey had given her body over to him. She lived with him here and at his home as well. Her face tightened ready to explode in another bout of tears and release. She nodded and reached out and cupped his face.

James took her hands and clasped them in his own. "Quit. Quit that horrible place. You don't belong there. You belong with me. Oh, how I wish I had met you two years ago. Things would have been so much simpler, but life doesn't always work to your advantage. But this I do know. I love you and I can't spend another second watching you self-destruct. We have to do something different, something better. You need to make a choice. Decide that you want a real life with me, and I will spend all my days trying to make it the best life possible for us."

Casey looked at him like he was crazy. His ideas and words didn't fit into anything she knew. He might as well been telling her to fly to the moon and he was. Casey stood up and went into her nightly routine of bath, a smoke, and then bed. James kept talking. He fueled the idea that what had just happened was unhealthy, that the idea of robbing a customer was desperate. That what they shared together was a real connection and founded in love. "Casey, your life doesn't suck. Not your whole life. Only the bad parts and you choose those every day. Choose something different. Choose something wonderful. Choose us. Believe in us. Trust in me."

Casey had turned off her emotions. She was stoic and cold. "You just don't want me to have any money."

"No, that's not it. I just don't want the woman that I love to be bouncing her head on the table and telling me she doesn't want to live anymore." James sat next to the tub as she soaked under a thick layer of bubbles. He reached in the water and fished out her hand then squeezed it. "I love you baby. We can make it together of that I am sure. And I want too. I want you in my life, every day. That's why I drive an hour every day to be with you. To show you how important you are to me and to love you. This life that you are living is filled with danger, pain, temptation and lies. Frankly, you aren't up to these challenges. But what you are is wonderful, loving, creative and kind. I want you to come home with me and leave all this behind."

"I'm not leaving my stuff here."

"We will come back for it. We will find a place in our home to put everything and make it ours." James squeezed her hand again.

"You don't want me to be happy."

James shook his head, "Contrary, I want you to be very happy. Look at you, do you call this happy? You survive by this terrible means. You don't have to. You chose to. It's easy, and it's not laborious, but it is sucking your soul out of you." Casey didn't want to hear the truth anymore. She just wanted to escape from him. Not from her life but from him telling her things she already knew. She got out of the tub and dried off and went into the living room. He followed her and kept comparing this life versus the weekend. The two environments were like night and day.

"Are you going to make me feel worse all night?" Casey eventually yelled.

"I am not the one making you feel this way. You are choosing to live this life, and I am tired and scared. I am not going to stay here and watch you kill yourself."

Casey lifted up her chin in defiance. It was moments like these that he knew she had some upbringing that instilled some fight in her. "You can't make me quit. I need this job."

"I won't make you do anything. You have to decide for yourself what is most important to you. Do you want this life that is eating at your soul and making you want to kill yourself? Or do you want to follow your heart and be loved by a man that puts you before everything?"

"You don't put me before everything."

"I do."

"You don't. You told me that your girls would always be first, and that we couldn't be a couple if they didn't like me."

"I did say that, and more importantly I meant it. But they don't just like you, they love you. We all do. And as long as they are children I will look out for their interests, and as long as they are children you will be second behind them, but you will still be before me. You will be more important to me than myself. I am not going to ever lie to you honey. We can do this if you can just trust a little bit."

Casey didn't want to hear any of this. It had been nearly three hours of the same old thing over and over and over. James wouldn't stop. She wasn't sure she wanted him too. He was painting out both lives, the one she lived now, and the one she had with him. James made one seem so filled with possibility and the other fraught with disaster. Three hours became four and four became eight, they eventually crawled in the bed and slept for four hours. James woke up first. Casey wondered if he slept at all.

James went into the kitchen and made some coffee. His face was tight now. His heart had hardened, and he wanted to save himself from this life. He looked at Casey and knew he loved her. He could feel it in every part of himself. She was not perfect, but she was perfect for him and he knew it. If only she would believe it. "What did you decide, honey?" James sat a cup of coffee down in front of her. She was wrapped up in her warm fluffy bathrobe. "What life do you want to live?"

Casey looked out the patio door and onto her deck. She could see the overflowing ash tray and all she wanted at that moment was to light another cigarette but she had run out after chain smoking the night before. "I have to get ready to go to work."

"You aren't going back Casey. You can't go back to that place."

"I have too. I need the money."

"What good is the money if you have to sell your soul?" James cleaned up the table and she went into the bedroom to dress. "I am leaving Casey. I am going home. Will you come with me?"

"I can't, I have to go to work aren't you listening to me?!" Casey was angry now, defensive.

"I hear you. Are you listening to me? I am not going to be a part of this life any longer. I am not going to wait around and see if you come home at night. If when you get here you want to kill yourself or complain for an hour about how all women are out to get you. I am not going to be a part of all this negativity. I have seen how wonderful you are, and I know that you can be happy but not here. I can't stay here Casey. I can't be in this life with you. You can come with me and choose a better future, or you can stay here and self-destruct." There he had said it. He didn't want to but he knew it had to be done, an ultimatum, not to her really but to himself. James had to make a choice and this was not the one he wanted. James couldn't live with himself everyday if he was going to have to stay worried and negative and fearful. If she wanted to be in his life, she would come with him. And if she wanted to live this dark fruitless life she would stay. "What do you say? Are you coming with me?"

"I'm going to work."

"Then good bye, honey. I really do love you."

"Will you be here when I come home?" she asked.

"No. I won't. I won't be coming back. I am not going to be a part of this world. I am not going to sit here and watch you kill yourself or become a whore or waste away into negativity. I am going home. Come with me or let me go." James picked up his keys and took her key off his key ring and set it on the table. Casey walked out of the bedroom and looked at him and then the key. James walked over and kissed her cheek and then he put his jacket on and walked towards the front door. "Good bye. I really did love you."

Casey ran to the door and slammed it shut then stood in front of him staring confused and scared. James stepped back and shook his head. "Please move. I am leaving. You don't want to be in my life; you want this instead."

"I don't want this at all. I want you. Please don't walk out on me."

"I am not walking out on you, love. I am leaving this bad life behind. You can choose to walk out of it with me. I am not leaving you; you are choosing to watch me go. Now please move." James couldn't hide his tear; he just let it fall across his face.

"I'll go with you. Just wait, let me get some things." James didn't believe her at first but she grabbed his hand and pulled him towards the bedroom. If she takes off her clothes, I am just leaving, he thought. She's not going to wile her way into what she wants this time. But Casey went into her closet and pulled out her bags and started filling them with clothes. James realized she was ready to go, but he didn't want her to change her mind, so he decided to help her. Together they packed as much as they could in five minutes and he led her out of the apartment like two kids eloping from her parent's house. James swiped the key from the table and picked up her phone and put it in his pocket.

When they got to the van, she paused and said she needed to go back in the house. "For what?" asked James?

"My phone. I forgot my phone." James put the van in gear and pulled out of the parking lot. "What are you doing, I want my phone."

"You don't need it."

"I do need it. I have to call them and tell them I'm not coming to work today."

"Today? It isn't about today. You aren't going back ever. And if you choose at some point to leave me, I know they will take you back. They use people willing to be used and sold. So fear not, selling sex will always be an option. But it is not an option for this life."

Casey was angry. She sat on her side arms crossed tightly. James drove ten minutes across town, and then Casey exploded, "You are kidnapping me!"

"Don't be absurd." James wondered why it took her so long. She obviously was having a panic attack.

"Take me home." James looked over at her as if to ask "really," but the answer would have been yes or she wouldn't have said it. He thought to turn around, but then he saw a Sheriff's car. James pulled up alongside the sheriff's car and dug down into his pockets. "I am not going back to your apartment. I am not going back to that life. I will go in a few days and help move your stuff out and bring it to our house and our new life. But if you want to quit before you even try, here is enough money for a cab to take you back, and you can stay with the sheriff till the cab gets here. But I'm not driving back and I'm not kidnapping you. If you want that life instead of a life with me, get out here." James looked out the window at the sheriff who seemed curiously disinterested. James made a hand motion to just wait a moment. Looking back at Casey, "What's it going to be, honey? Love? Or do you want me to get your bag out." She sat there staring out the front window.

In a soft voice of resignation, "Just take me home."

"Mine or yours?" James put his hand on the door opener.

Casey rolled her neck around and then took a deep breath, "Yours."

James didn't smile on the outside, but he felt much relieved on the inside. Looking over at the deputy, he smiled and shrugged his shoulders, then he put the van in gear and drove Casey to her new home. James was determined to make it work out for them.

When they pulled into the front yard, he looked over at Casey. Reaching out he took her hand and squeezed it. "From this day forward this is not my house anymore. This is our house. This is our home. To me it is just a place to sleep and store my stuff. Stuff that I really don't even care about. What I do care about is you. You are my home and my family now. Where ever you are is where my love and attention will be. Welcome home, Casey. Thank you for choosing us."

"I have only two demands," began Casey. James heart stopped. She walked right up to him and stared him in the eyes. "I will not" she said emphatically, "tolerate bad pizza." James sighed a breath of relief and realized he had not been breathing. "And " she continued, "you can never call me worthless."

"I never will," James promised.

It got easier quickly

"...because that's what makes the flowers grow."

James woke up the next morning and Casey was asleep beside him. He lay there staring at her. She had chosen their life together. She lived here now. He smiled. She wants to be here with him. He thought himself a sap as he wiped away a tear running across his cheek. This was his second chance at happiness. Casey made him happy already, and now that she had escaped from the club he thought they had a chance at a real life. But he wasn't deluded, he knew she was going to need some outside encouragement. She was going to need some support and some friends. He had no clue how he was going to make it all work but he was certain that unlike his ex-wife, Casey wanted to be his partner in life. She wanted to help herself and improve. Together he could see a wonderful future. Two people that believed in one another. James slipped out of bed and made her breakfast and coffee.

Their first day was filled with tears and her fears that she might not be secure. How was she going to make it all work. Casey vocalized as if it were going to all be up to her. James comforted her and consoled her. She would do well for a while and then have another panic attack. James stayed focused and as positive as he could be without seeming fake. He was sure that it would work, she just needed some time to warm up to this idea. Wednesday would pass and she would survive. Thursday would make all the difference in the world.

Casey wanted some things from her apartment that she had forgotten. She wanted to tell the strip club that she hadn't quit that she would be back. She insisted that she had been kidnapped. James told her the phone in the kitchen worked and the front door opens from the inside. She argued that she needed her phone, but he insisted that she didn't. "You don't have any friends that you talk to ever and the majority of your contacts are customers. But you aren't going to do that work anymore. You are starting a new life, a better one. You need stuff? Make me a list."

Casey made a list and he drove an hour to get her things. He looked around her apartment and hoped that soon it would be empty and she would stay with him. He gathered her things plus a few extras like her paintings from the wall and brought them home.

He got back in time to pick her up and they went to school and picked up his younger children. They wanted to go to Chick-Filet and play and that seemed a good place for them to hear the good news. While he ordered food Casey played with them in the kid's play area. She was great with them and they loved her. She climbed and chased and slide down the slide. They loved her energy and she loved their attention.

When James called them all to the table, he said he had an announcement, "Casey has come to live with us. We are planning on being a couple for a long time. What do you guys think?" Their faces exploded with joy. Casey looked like she was going to explode as well, they bounced on her and hugged her and she seemed happily overwhelmed. James calmed them all down and they had a wonderful family dinner.

Casey didn't do well every day, but that was to be expected. The first thing they needed to do was to find her some professional help for her panic attacks. Friday they drove around to the free mental health clinics and finally was directed to the appropriate people to schedule an appointment. They would have to wait a week but she was in the system now and they had a lot of hope for future progress. James did most of the talking but when he handed her the phone she talked freely and expressed that she really wanted some help. James didn't want to distract her but when she looked out the side window he placed his hand on her thigh. She didn't look back but she did intertwine her fingers in his. He was so very proud of her. She had asked for help before but told him that people just shuffled her away. He had stuck with it and pushed through all the barriers and side tracks. It took the better part of two days to really get to where they needed to be. But now, they had an opportunity and she took it. And he held her close and told her how much it meant to him to see her taking control of her destiny.

The days would get better quickly. February would warm up quickly and the improved weather also helped with improved attitudes. Without the negative in her life she was far less cynical. When she realized that the world wasn't tumbling down but instead that each day was filled with sunshine and laughter and love, she rebounded quickly. Early in the week James took her out to explore some of her new world. He drove through town and country and pointed out where he went to school, where his family was from, and places that had certain memories for him. One of those was the washout. James grandmother had talked about how people used to come when she was a little girl in the 1930s. James always thought it was a beautiful place and he enjoyed sharing it with Casey. She really opened up and became the wonderful woman that would dominate her personality for the next several months.

People were already enjoying the washout when they arrived. She didn't seem too interested in socializing with any of them until a horseman stopped and let his majestic animal idle about.

James noticed Casey looking at the horse and took a chance, "Would you like me to take you horseback riding?"

"That would be fun." Casey smiled and looked over at him.

"Do you know how to ride?"

He could see Casey rolling her eyes even behind those sunglasses. "Of course I do."

"Why don't you ask him to let you ride. People around here are very friendly." Casey looked at him like he had lost his mind. You don't just walk up to somebody and say 'hey can I drive your car, sleep with your wife, ride your horse.' Well, most people don't do that but James wasn't most people. James walked across the stream and started talking to the horseman. He didn't waste any time before asking him could Casey ride the horse around a bit. The man introduced himself as 'Cowboy' and told James that the horse was so well trained that kids jumped on him all the time and no one thought nothing of it. James waved for Casey to come over and she made her way across the stream to them.

Casey is a little short but she has so much spirit and she was not timid in the least. With just a bit of help she was up in the saddle and in full control. She rode off down a trail she had never been on before. James thought of the metaphor and wondered how apt this experience was. Casey returned in about ten minutes with a smile so wide you could tell she felt free and empowered. James made a mental note that they needed to do this again.

Casey was bursting with joy after her ride. She walked up behind James and took his hand. He thought it might have been the first time she did it first. He would soon come to find that she always wanted to hold his hand. He loved that she did.

They walked the winding path back to the van and drove towards home a different way. James pointed out a few things and then pulled the van over. "I have always meant to stop here and never have." He got out of the van and she followed along with him. They didn't walk far they just explored together. Casey had not stopped smiling for over an hour. She truly seemed to be having a wonderful time. The last few days had been emotional and hard but now she was warming up to her new life and forgetting about the one she left behind.

She walked ahead of him and into the trees. He intentional slowed down so that he could watch her explore. He loved how she studied everything, the trees, the flowers, the dry leaves and the mushroom. She shared his love of detail. She didn't mind squatting down to study a plant closer or squinting to examine an insect on a tree. Her curiosity was like his own. She was amazed by her world and he was amazed by her.

Everything she did that day seemed to please her. Her smile was contagious and her laughter intoxicating. It was the longest he had ever seen her happy without a break in her smile.

James was happy too. He couldn't believe that she had chosen him. He knew that she said she wanted to marry him but then when she acted out he wondered if she was just telling him what he wanted to hear. But now, he was sure she was in love with him, just being in the same room with him put a smile on her face and that made him smile and his heart swell.

The Healing Begins

"Never wait till tomorrow to show them you love them today." – Daniel Orr

"Why?" asked Casey.

"Why what." Replied James rhetorically.

Casey looked at him playing on his computer. She hadn't really cared he was playing because she was playing on his iPad. They did this often, him doing one thing she doing another but they did it together in close proximity.

"Tell me?" Casey demanded playfully.

"I'm sorry, honey. Could you be a little more vague." James turned around in his chair and looked at her stretched across the bed. She was wearing his shirt and it was too big on her but he loved to see her do it.

"Are you happy with me here?" She looked worried. She was up and down since she had left her stripper life behind.

Sometimes having panic attacks and crying spells but no more disassociations. Most importantly her negativity seemed washed away. She was more in amazement that life could be so simple, so good.

"I have never been happier. Truly." James leaned forward in his chair and reached out and took her ankle and stroked her foot. "I did not even know what happiness felt like until you came into my life. You make every moment wonderful."

"Why? Why do you want me?" Casey seemed genuinely concerned.

"What?" James snorted, "You want a list?"

Casey tilted her head and her eyes squinted into concern, "Yes." She said tenderly, meekly.

James realized that she needed reinforcement. He began with a big smile, "OK my love. I will make you a list." He spun around in his computer chair and typed out a list and then hit print. Casey tried to peek several times but he would minimize the screen and shoo her away. When he was done, he removed it from the printer and spun the chair around to face the bed again. "Here, let me read it to you."

Casey jumped up and bounded into his lap. She did not land softly nor graceful and nearly tilted the chair over. James wrapped his arm around her middle and tried to lift her. She responded by bracing her foot on the bed and pressing against him hard. She took the paper from him and held it out, James began to read it to her.

1. The Sound of Your Laughter
2. Deep Dimples in your smile
3. Cuddles
4. White Teeth
5. Artistic Talent
6. Spicy Food Eater
7. Walks around Naked
8. Soft Eyes
9. Intelligent

10. Educated
11. Snarky
12. Pony Tails
13. Well Dressed
14. Plays Rough
15. Surrenders softly
16. Angelic Face
17. Beautiful Body
18. Likes to watch her stretch
19. Laughs at her morning hack
20. House Coat, socks, and coffee
21. Likes day trips
22. Gentle touch
23. Likes Band Practice
24. Trusts Me
25. Amazing, intoxicating smile
26. Silly
27. Open
28. Bourbon girl
29. Water Slides
30. Boats
31. Excellent Hygiene
32. Social Drinker
33. Photographer

34. Painter
35. Search for knowledge
36. Longing for happiness
37. Intolerance for stupidity
38. Vocalizes Emotions
39. Pasta chef
40. Loves her dainty hands and feet
41. Strong athletic legs
42. Reads books
43. Day Dreams
44. Playful
45. Ice Cream
46. Uses Internet
47. Kick Boxing
48. Sleeps through my snoring
49. Likes it on the floor
50. Passive
51. Vents her feelings
52. Has goals
53. Strong Independence
54. Sacrifice job for her dream
55. Likes Me
56. Eats with chop sticks
57. Cracks knuckles

58. Sexy and playful
59. Likes hiking
60. Likes posing for the camera
61. Horseback riding
62. Willing to explore new things
63. Loves me

Casey finished reading before he finished reading aloud. She twisted in the chair and looked at him studying his face to measure truthfulness. "Really?" she asked in a whisper.

"I love you, woman. All of you."

TRAGEDY, FEBRUARY 2011

"To part is the lot of all mankind. The world is a scene of constant leave-taking, and the hands that grasp in cordial greeting today, are doomed ere long to unite for the last time, when the quivering lips pronounce the word - 'Farewell" – R.M. Ballantyne

The beginning of something wonderful was about to occur. Casey started her counseling sessions and even granted James a HIPPA to be a part of her sessions. The psychiatrist diagnosed her with Generalized Anxiety Disorder also known as GAD, chronic paranoia and mild depression.

Casey had commented more than a few times that the girls at the club hated her and they probably did. The women in the strip club were very catty and immature and they were in competition for the various men's money. So a pretty girl was stiff competition for the other women who were not so fortunate. But there was more to her belief that women didn't like her. She had made a few comments that no matter where she went in life, shopping, job hunting, work, church, everywhere, Casey believed that women singled her out for persecution. James made the mistake of laughing at one of her comments. She flew hot and insisted that she knew what had happened.

"Really honey?" James began to dig his own grave, "You really think these women have secret meetings to plot and make sure your life fails and is miserable?"

"Yes" she retorted quickly and she meant it. James looked stunned and realized that his jovial statement was not taken the way it was intended. Casey noticed his discomfort and her face softened. "They really do." She remarked softly.

James listened to Casey tell him about her life. How her high school boyfriend had taken her virginity but then left her disillusioned and it would be a couple of years and into college before she let anyone that close again.

She talked about her last boyfriend who had been a prominent chef and a local celebrity. She described a life of culinary exploration and happy times. But she didn't go into a lot of detail and there were no favorite moments, at least not in the way he told stories. She had a very generalized and separated view of her past. She talked about how she felt during these times but not so much what she actually did or didn't do. In the end of the chef story, she claimed he spent more times with his friends than with her. And when he started cheating on her, she cheated on him and it all soon came to a close. Casey did not indicate that it was mean or hostile, just that it didn't work out.

One thing James noticed is that with each story she told him, she became a little more comfortable telling him the next story. They spent most every day in the same room. Different rooms at different times but where ever he went she followed. The second week together he realized they had hardly been apart at all. He realized also they he didn't mind, in fact he loved that she wanted to be right beside him. He loved that she had the need to reach out and touch him. She did so lovingly and often.

Casey came to James her face all twisted. "What is it honey?" The pain was too much and her eyes welled with tears but none fell. She showed him her email and he read that her grandfather had died. There would be a service for him in his home town in New York.

James wrapped his arms around her and they rocked together on the bedside. "Now I wish we had gone to see him like I suggested in December. I am so sorry honey. I know you loved him so much. Let me get Jamie to stay at her mom's and I'll take you to say good bye to your grandfather." Casey jerked away from him. She looked around the room like a frightened animal.

"I'm not going." James approached her slowly and took her back into his arms. He held her close and they rocked back and forth. This was not the kind of anxiety she needed.

James held her tight and whispered, "Let's go say good bye." Casey shook her head and James refused to let her go. She seemed to find comfort in his embrace like he wrapped her in security. "I never got a chance to meet him. You made him sound wonderful. I'll drive. You just keep me awake and alert."

Casey didn't like this idea at all. James was sure that she didn't need to have anything to regret for. He was going to find a way to get her to go say goodbye but he had to do so without pushing her. She needed to realize that she wanted to go.

"Had he been sick?" James asked her?

She said that he had but she also thought that he had made some improvements. She admitted that she hadn't talked to him in a while. James went into the kitchen and when he returned she had found some pictures from a vacation to Florida a little over a year ago. He seemed pretty healthy in the photos.

"I know that this was a big shock, but I will tell you that it was horrible watching my grandmother die slowly. Especially when I knew I was the one killing her." Casey glanced up him in confusion. "She had Alzheimer's for a very long time. She had been reduced to less than an animal. There was no part of her that was her old self, her true self." James fought back a tear, "It cemented for me that there was no active god. There was no other woman who praised god more or thanked him more. And she spent the last seven years turning into a mindless monster.

"When she had her stroke, she was paralyzed on her right side and she couldn't swallow." James sat down on the bed and turned his back to Casey, "They said she would live but they would have to teach her to swallow again. I told them that she couldn't remember your name for more than 15 seconds how would they ever teach her anything." James had tears rolling across his cheeks, "I told them to stop feeding her or giving her water. I told them to feed her meds so she wouldn't hurt but to starve and dehydrate her to death. If she couldn't feed herself on her own then they were to let her die."

Casey slide up behind him and wrapped one arm around his middle. "Hospice was supposed to ensure that the orders were carried out but the nurses were sneaking her water. She should have died in six days but it would take nearly thirteen. My grandfather caught them trying to feed her once. When I talked to the nursing staff one of them called me a murderer. They didn't realize she had been dead for years in her mind."

Casey pressed herself hard into his back. She put her arms around him and squeezed him. "You would drive me all the way to New York?"

"I would do anything for you honey. One day I hope you will believe me."

"I do." Casey hugged him some more and then she got up and went into the kitchen and made him a glass of water. Returning she sat down beside him, "We can go. If you want to."

James looked at her, "We can go if you want too. I think you should. If your family gets in the way, just come to me and I will divert them away. You have nothing to fear from them while I am with you."

On the way there she described who she expected to be in attendance. She was particular concerned that she needed to avoid one of her aunts. She was correct in guessing that her half-sister nor mother would come. James could understand why the half-sister might not want to go but her mother? Her mother had not divorced her father, he had died in an industrial accident. James couldn't relate to her not being supportive of that family. Maybe he assumed too much, but he would have thought that Casey's dad's family would have been the support mechanism upon his death. But that would not seem to be the case.

Everyone was in mourning. Casey's grandfather was very well respected and a large group had come to give their respects. When James and Casey walked up the steps, people stopped talking to one another. Casey looked so sad and terrified. Her uncle was handicapped but when he saw her he immediately came to her and wrapped his arms around her. He gushed with love and admiration.

Casey did not introduce James to anyone. A few people would come and introduce themselves and when she was standing next to him she only remarked, "He's a friend who drove me up here." James heart sank. Just a friend he wondered. He knew she didn't want to come. He knew that she neither liked nor trusted any of these family members. He watched them and looked for any sign of them being terrible people but he saw none. Still the older generation put Casey very much at unease. They hugged her and talked to her and she looked like she just wanted to escape. James stood at a distance and watched. Casey never even looked for him in the room. She stood with her arms wrapped around her chest defensively. She looked like she might have been trying to zombie out of herself. When James noticed that, he went to her and took her arm and led her outside for some fresh air.

Casey lite a cigarette and then hid behind the cars to smoke it. She had not smoked since coming to his house, but he wasn't going to point it out now. James did wonder where the cigarette had come from but that was a very little concern. Casey looked at the cars and their license plates. She remarked who she thought owned each one. When she crushed out the cigarette James took her into his arms and kissed her forehead.

"Listen, we came all this way for you to say good bye to your grandfather. You are doing great in there. You seem uncomfortable but you are surviving. It will all be over soon. We can go after or we can go to the restaurant that people are talking about. I will leave it up to you." Casey looked up him and smiled just a little bit. It was the only smile she had had today.

They went back in the funeral hall and Casey went up and sat with her extended family. Her brother walked up to James and thanked him for bringing his sister. James wanted to tell him that she was living with him and they talked of marriage. James had a thousand questions but this was not the time nor place for them. He shook his hand and then he found a place to sit near the back. One by one the family took turns telling stories about their father, Casey's grandfather. They mentioned Casey's father a couple of times and James wondered what her life would have been like had he lived. Watching them all they were not strikingly different, but they were not like his own family.

After the ceremony James learned that Yankees didn't bury their dead right away. Apparently the ground is too hard and they put the deceased on ice until the ground thaws. He gave that concept more thought than it probably deserved. He imagined a ritual where they build a funeral pyre and cremate outdoors it made him snicker. And just as he did, Casey's uncle came up to him and offered his hand. James smiled and introduced himself. Her uncle wouldn't let go. He was shorter than James but they had the same build. He pulled at James hand to make him come closer. "Casey is a very special girl. She's had a rough life. You be a good friend to her. Thank you for bringing her to us. I love Casey, if she ever needs me you call me." James nodded that he would. James wondered what all that meant, obviously there was something going on he didn't know about. Maybe she would tell him when she was ready.

The family gathered around and took a group photo. They seemed pleased she was there.

When everyone started piling into the restaurant Casey opened up a little. As her cousins arrived she abandoned James and mingled and talked and shared. He didn't mind. This was the first time he had ever seen her with friends or family of her own. She was always with him and did not seem to have any other social connections. To see her interact with her cousins made him feel very warm inside, hopeful.

As the evening progressed, a few of her family members came and introduced themselves to James. Some it seemed just wondered who he was and others wondered how he and Casey were associated. James didn't give out any information. She had referred to him as 'just a friend who drove me up here.' That had hurt him a little but he had made mistakes too like when he laughed at her paranoia. If she wasn't ready to share with people he professed to hate then it really didn't matter too much as long as he believed that she loved him.

Just before they left, the last group they visited with were just friends of the family. She seemed very comfortable with them, more so than with the blood relatives. She never really introduced James but did include him in the conversation and at one point reached out and squeezed his forearm. He imagined that was a very large leap for her.

When the last good bye had been said, they got in the van and drove a while to get a head start on the way back tomorrow.

In the hotel room, Casey undressed

and started the shower. She walked over to him naked and hugged him. "I want to bath alone. Is that ok?"

"Of course it is. Today is a sad day of goodbyes. You don't owe me, Casey. I am here to support you because I love you." She smiled at him and went into the bathroom. He crawled into the bed. It was very cold in yankee land. James remembered now why he hated Chicago so much.

Hershey Pennsylvania

"All you need is love. But a little chocolate now and then doesn't hurt." – *Charles M. Schulz*

As they drove south, James passed a sign and exclaimed, "No way!"

Casey looked out the window but didn't see anything. "What is it?" she seemed almost frightened.

"We just passed a sign that said Hershey!" James was like a kid all of a sudden. "I love chocolate, and we are next to the mother lode!"

Casey snorted. Apparently she had been her before it was no big deal. But it was to James, "there is no way I can be this close and not go look." James looked at Casey for approval but she seemed very disinterested. James suddenly felt selfish and self-loathing. This was a sad time for her and here he was bouncing around like a child. "We don't have to go. I just got excited."

"We can go if you want to." Casey smiled him weakly.

"Really? Are you sure? It would be a waste to drive right by and not see it? How far out of the way is it?" Casey said she didn't know and they stopped by a gas station and asked. "15 minutes?" James had a devilish grin. Casey laughed at him. James handed her a piece of chocolate he had bought in the store. Casey broke half of it off and stuck it in his mouth. She smiled wide and for the first time today.

Now you put a fat man in a candy store and you get a smile. You put a fat man in a chocolate factory and oh my god! James had programmed automations his whole life and here was the Willie Wonka Wonderland of machines making candy. They took the tour and James pointed out all the machinery he was familiar with. Casey didn't really seem to care but she did seem amused by his childish enthusiasm. They dressed up in cook's attire and went with a group to design and create their very own Chocolate Bar.

James made the James-0-licious and she invented the Casey Crunch! Together they enjoyed a couple of hours of nonsense and play. It had placed them way behind in getting home so they stayed an extra night. This time however, Casey didn't want to shower alone and they didn't go to sleep until very late. James didn't even notice how cold it was.

When they arrived back in town they brought with them a treasure trove of chocolate. The star of the booty was a five pound Hershey's candy bar. They took it to the school and had the teachers of James kids split it between the two classes. It fed them all with some left over. It didn't take too many nosey teachers before all that was gone too.

When the kids came home, Casey gave them giant Hershey Kisses and smaller candy bars for them personally. They hugged and laughed but wouldn't dare break their chocolate open. So James went and got more from Wal-Mart. Casey accused him of spoiling them too much. James agreed with her.

The Happiest Place on Earth

"Love is that condition in which the happiness of another person is essential to your own." – Robert A. Heinlein, <u>Stranger in a Strange Land</u>

James watched her transform a little more every day. He had been right, taken away from her world of dark desires, lost souls, stress and lies she had flourished. In the beginning he had sought out to find the zombie girl that everyone had discounted. Upon finding her, he immediately saw a soul in distress and sought only to make her smile.

Now, he saw her smile every day. Her laughter filled the rooms of their home and every corner of his heart. She seemed as if she had lived there forever. Her presence was the element that made the house a home and it was filled with love.

James could hardly contain himself, he wanted to tell her every minute that he loved her more than the minute before. He could not recall in all of his years having ever been so happy. The two of them just seemed to have everything in common. Even the things that separated them were complimentary. They loved making each other feel important. As February was coming to a close, an opportunity arose. James asked Jamie would it be ok if he asked Casey to marry him. All the other children he was sure about but Jamie seemed happy sometimes and distant others. When he asked her, her face lit up "Yes daddy. I think that would be great."

"I want to take her somewhere special and ask her, someplace that she can always remember." Jamie smiled she knew what a romantic sap her daddy was and she knew that he was going to do something big. "When you go to your mother's this weekend, I would appreciate it if you let me leave early and you just take yourself over after school. I will see you Monday when you come home from school."

Jamie nodded and agreed. She leapt into his arms and hugged him tightly. "I am very happy for you daddy. You deserve this."

James gave his daughter money for gas and the weekend. "If you need more just tell your mom you need gas money. It isn't necessary to tell her that I already gave you some. And there is always the emergency jar on the wine cabinet if you need more money." James wrapped her up tightly in his arms. "Thanks Jamie. This means a lot to me. I never knew what happiness truly was until Casey came into my life."

Jamie left for school and James started a pot of coffee. The aroma filled the air and he heard Casey walk into the bathroom down the hall. He turned around and looked at the mirror. This was going to be slightly spontaneous. He liked impulsive but not expensive and impulsive. This had elements of both and yet it didn't. He did not come to this decision lightly and he had fantasized about it in his head now for three months.

James looked over at the calendar and realized that today was his ex-wife's birthday. He wondered if that was some secret life message that one door was being sealed shut forever and another door was opening to a bright and better future.

Casey came into the kitchen and held her arms in the air. "Crack my back," a common request. James stood behind her and wrapped his arms around her then lifted her up until he heard a series of pops. Setting her back down on the ground she looked almost dizzy and her face beamed with love and admiration.

James wrapped his arms around her and pulled her close to him. "I love you."

She smiled and kissed him lightly on the lips. "I love you too."

"Would you like to go on an adventure? Just the two of us? I always wanted to do the Bohemian thing and just drive a little sleep in the van and visit a couple of places."

She looked perplexed but interested. "Did you have a place in mind?"

"Uh, maybe. Florida. We could save money by sleeping in the van and then we could do more stuff. I always dreamed of this kind of vacation I just never had anyone adventurous enough to do it with."

"Ok. I'm good with it. When do you want to go?"

"Now, but we have things to do first." James poured her a cup of coffee and they ran around that day getting things ready. When Jamie came home from school, he gave her a big hug and told her to call him if she needed anything. Then he and Casey left for Florida.

It was only a nine hour drive slightly shorter than the drive they had took to New York earlier in the month. Casey was the disc jockey and used the iPad to play an assortment of songs as they travelled. The conversations flowed out from them and they talked about life and their pasts. He loved hearing about her passions. She had experienced things with initiative all her own he liked that about her. She was very dependent but she was also very adventurous. He loved the look of discovery that dominated her face whenever he took her someplace new. She studied everything to minute details. He loved to watch her dissect the world and suck the very essence of things out of it. His passion for knowledge and understanding was so close to hers. They seemed to like to argue and then look up ideas and facts and share what they found. Sometimes she was very rigid in what she believed even in the face of facts she discovered on her own. James was much more fluid and often just merged ideas and concepts giving them weight in his mental stores.

The drive down was filled with laughter and he loved the way she needed to reach out and scratch his arm or touch his leg. It wasn't sexual, it was just letting him know she was next to him and then she was happy being there. His heart overflowed and he knew he was doing the right thing.

They began to become exhausted just after entering Florida. James decided that instead of driving all the way there and be too tired to enjoy themselves they should stop and take a nap and then finish the journey in the morning. Casey agreed and they pulled into a dark corner of a very nice Florida Rest Area. The house had a terracotta roof and an arcade along the length. Casey pointed it out and James acknowledged that he loved it too. Then admitted he didn't know it was called an arcade, only arches. Casey was quick to tell him that she had studied architectures and he could doubt her if he liked but she was right. James thought she must be getting tired and grumpy. "I wasn't questioning you, honey. I said I didn't know that. Why would I?"

They threw the bench seat down in the

back of the van and put blankets up against the back glass to block a street light. Now James figured they were going to snore, stretch and resume but Casey had to get 'comfortable' and then she snuggled against him but that wasn't comfortable. Then they shifted to be parallel and then anti-parallel and then spooned and then James sat up and leaned the middle seat all the way back. Then he started giggling.

"What?" asked Casey.

"I suck at this roughing it. I thought it would fun but now I think I am too used to being comfortable. Let's find a better place to sleep than a van. Maybe I am just too old to be a Bohemian."

Casey laughed at him. "We don't have to stay anywhere nice. We are just going to sleep for four hours. Find one of those cheap motels." So they drove about fifteen minutes and rented the first place they found. Entering the room they looked at the walls and then each other.

James threw the bedspread off the bed onto the floor. "At least the sheets look washed and clean. I have slept in worse places."

Casey ran her fingernails across his bare chest. "I just want to sleep next to you." There were two twin beds but they only used one of them.

In the morning they got some coffee and drove to Disney World. Casey had never been and James was on his twenty-ninth visit. He could not wait to see the wonder and amazement on her face. They decided to do the Animal Kingdom first.

James loved Disney. When they walked through the gate an attendant greeted them with, "Welcome home!" James looked at Casey and knew that where ever she was that was his home because that was where his heart resides. He held out his hand and she entwined her fingers in his and then bounced against his side and lay her head on his shoulder for a few steps. He could not have been any happier.

The first things he insisted on doing was to get Casey an autograph book so that she could have the characters of Disney sign it and she could have a memory to carry with her for the rest of her life. He recalled how barren her apartment had been. No sign of a past life. He recalled all the bad relationships she described and how they seemed to lack wonder and excitement. He could not wait to begin this new chapter in his life. Casey looking happier than ever and armed with an autograph book they consumed Disney's Magic Kingdom.

"The wonderful thing about Tiggers are Tiggers are a wonderful thing. Their head's are made out of rubber. Their tails are made out of springs. They bounce and bounce and bounce and bounce and have such fun fun fun. The wonderful thing about Tigger's is I'm the only one!" James sang loud and probably got the words wrong but he didn't care he loved Tigger and Casey looked at him like a lunatic singing amongst the line of people waiting for an autograph. She did not seem to like the close proximity to people or the waiting but once she got to the front and Tigger grabbed a hold of her she might as well of been a five year old girl. Tigger will do that too you.

As much as Casey had not wanted to wait in line for Tigger's autograph, she did want to wait in line for Eeyore's. Walking up to him she handed him the pen and dropped it. Eeyore looked down at the pen downtrodden and Casey burst into laughter. Eeyore turned around and moped away to stand alone. Casey looked at James. "What did you to Eeyore?" chided James.

"Nothing!" exclaimed Casey and Eeyore turned around and returned to Casey. This time she placed the pen firmly in his hand and he signed her autograph book.

They hopped a safari tour and rode around the park looking at all the animals. He knew how much she loved animals and she stayed fascinated going from one exhibit to another.

James didn't even flinch. Casey had this squeak that meant a wide assortment of things. It could mean that she dropped a paper towel and had to bend over to get it. It could mean that she couldn't reach the remote control and this was her desperation cry for James to walk two rooms over and hand it to her. It could mean that the ice maker got stuck and there was no ice. So in the grand scheme of things, James did not get too overly concerned when he heard her squeak. It just so happened that this time he should of looked quickly. As they were looking at glass figurines, on of Disney's squirrels decided that Casey was in his path and rather than run around he just ran over her. She was dancing around in a fit and people next to her were laughing in astonishment. "I saw him too!" one man shouted.

James listened as she described the three

second drive by the squirrel. He loved how excited she became and how she giggled and laughed. It was intoxicating.

James could not wait for nightfall and the opportunity he desired. On their meager budget they finished up Animal Kingdom around four and went to the hotel room and showered. She looked like she wanted to show her appreciation but he kissed her and hugged her, "We have too much to do here. Mandatory fun and the clock is ticking. We have the rest of our lives to love one another." James took her hand and they re-entered the park at Disney's Magic Kingdom.

Space Mountain was a must but daylight was fleeting so they made their way to the Safari Boat Ride. James chuckled, because he knew the dialogue almost by heart. It changed from one captain to another but in as many visits as he had been a part of he knew most every line.

They rode rides and saw exhibits and the night was progressing far too quickly there was so much more to do. His normal vacations were four days but he had to pack it all into to two this time. But he had only come for one purpose. And it was getting closer.

Tom Sawyer's Island wasn't nearly as fun in the darkness and James disability was starting to make him feel nauseated. He refused to tell Casey or she would want to go back to the hotel and he wanted her to experience as much as she could. But his body wasn't going to let him and so he lead her towards the exit of the park. Only to discover in a little sidewalk cove Mickey and Minnie Mouse signing autographs. What better prelude to what he was about to ask than to have Disney's Premier Love Birds her signing autographs.

They waited a long twenty minutes to get to the front of the line but just before their turn, Minnie's bow fell off her head. She retreated into some mysterious anteroom to get fixed up and left James and Casey at the front of the line. Now everyone got about a minute of time with the characters as they posed took pictures and shook hands and hugged. But it was fast and furious and very scripted. But with Minnie missing, Mickey decided to break bad. He reached out and took Casey's hand and lead her out to the greeting area. He began by bowing low and kissing her hand and then he danced about playfully flirting with her. James stood by laughing and Mickey waved him off as if he was about to run away with Casey. The interaction lasted more than five minutes and ended only when Minnie returned and saw Mickey flirting with Casey. Minnie stood at the entrance gate, arms folded and tapping her foot. When Mickey saw her standing there he immediately began behaving and lead Casey over to James and then went to hug Minnie. She snuffed him. Everyone laughed.

Mickey came over and took James hand and lead him to Minnie then all four of them danced briefly and hugged.

It could not have been better had he planned it. Casey walked away laughing and excited and filled with mirth. James imagined his whole life filled with the joy of her laughter and the sound of her voice. He wanted to live with her enthusiasm. All he had ever hoped for was to see her smile and now she was all he dreamed of, except she wasn't a dream. She was there every morning and every night. In front of Cinderella's Castle James stopped and took her hands.

"Casey Ann Hobbes, I say your whole name because I want you to know that I am talking exclusively to you. I never imagined a life so full or so happy was ever this possible. I brought us here because I wanted to ask you this in a magical place because of all the magic you have brought to my life. Casey, I hope I am what you want forever because I want you to be my wife."

Casey looked at him and her eyes welled up with a tear. She studied his face over and again like she didn't believe he was really asking her to marry him. But his eyes were welling up as well. His face had been serious but now a smile crept across his lips. "Here in the happiest place on earth make me the happiest man on earth and tell me 'yes, you want to be my wife.'"

"Yes," she paused, then "Yes!" smiled Casey and she kissed him joyfully.

This was not the end of their story, only the beginning. There would be trials in their life, but there would be much more laughter and joy. She had made him the happiest man in the world, and he was going to spoil her terribly.